KAYLA WREN

Extra Credit

First published by Black Cherry Publishing 2021

First edition

ISBN: 978-1-914242-07-6

Cover art by Black Cherry Book Covers

This book was professionally typeset on Reedsy.
Find out more at reedsy.com

Contents

Keep in touch with Kayla!

Want to hear about new releases, sales, bonus content and other cool stuff? Sign up for Kayla's newsletter at www.kaylawrenauthor.com/newsletter!

Prologue

Two Years Earlier

I leave him in the cloakroom. The warm, muggy air of the bar washes over me as I step outside, blinking in the dim light. My eyes grew used to the shadows over the last twenty minutes, shut away in there in the dark. I smooth my dress over my hips, tuck my hair behind my ear, and wipe the corner of my mouth with the tip of my finger as I walk back to the bar. My heeled boots echo on the wooden floorboards and I swing my hips with each step, hiding a smile.

I can still taste him.

Normally, on a night like this, I wouldn't stop where I just did. In another cloakroom, with a different strange man, I might rise up from my knees and let him touch me back. Let him put his hands and mouth on me; let him try to make me call out his name.

His name. *Gideon.* Strong and classic, like a medieval knight. It suits him.

For some reason, though, I balked. Tonight, when this particular man reached for me to return the favor, I skirted out of arm's reach. Not because I didn't want him—god, I wanted him—but because of the sadness in his eyes back at the bar. He'd stared into the bottom of his glass like there had better be some damn answers in there, because if not, life was too cruel.

So I stepped away. I didn't want to make this about me. Call me crazy, but I wanted to give him something. A man like that, a man with bottomless sorrow in his hazel eyes… he deserves to feel good.

I made him feel good, alright.

My phone buzzes in the small bag hanging against my hip. I dig it out, swiping over the screen, scanning all the missed texts and voice mails. All the usual suspects are there: my roommates; my mom and stepdad; my older brother and cousin. Everyone is freaking out because Little Lucy didn't answer her phone for five freaking minutes.

They don't get it. I'm grown up; I have been for a long time. I left home for college two years ago and I haven't looked back since. I *love* the big city—the anonymity, the chance to remake myself every day if I choose.

I'm a damn adult, and if I want a night alone for once, a night to be a stranger in a dive bar… I can have that. It's nobody's goddamn business.

Gideon. The name floats across my brain again, unbidden. What kind of name is that? Is it English? French? I should have asked where he was from. What he does for a living. Gotten to know him, just a tiny bit.

No. A door slams shut in my brain, the echo reverberating through my body. I'm not here to get to know guys. Not here to *risk* anything, to make myself vulnerable. I'm here for fun.

Gideon.

There was a slight accent to his voice. A growl that started deep in his chest. I heard it again when he came, his head tipped up to the ceiling and his fingers wound through my hair.

Gideon.

He's the most fun I've ever had.

Chapter One

My hand shakes as I raise it, curling my fingers into a fist. I hesitate outside the door, other students throwing me weird looks as they pass behind me in the hall. The posters and fliers pinned to the noticeboards flutter as they walk past, and the shabby gray carpet muffles their steps. The heater clanks and groans against the wall, rattling its pipes, and condensation beads the window.

I suck in a deep breath. Count to three. Stay frozen, my fist floating in mid air. Outside, a pigeon flutters down to land clumsily on the windowsill, puffing up its feathers and watching me with those beady, orange eyes.

I clear my throat, wiping my damp forehead with the back of my raised hand. The pigeon cocks its head.

"Oh, shut up," I mutter, thumping on the door before I can think twice. I've overcompensated in my nerves, knocking so hard the door rattles on its hinges, and heat floods my cheeks.

It's not too late. The corridor isn't that long; I could make it around the corner if I sprint now...

The handle turns, the door tugging open, and *he* stands there.

Gideon.

No—*not* Gideon. Professor Warwick. The man who holds my future in his palms.

The man who hates me.

"Hi." It comes out in a squeak. I clear my throat. "Uh. Hi. Do you have a minute, Professor?"

He tilts his head, dropping his gaze from my heeled ankle boots, up my woolen tights to my sweater dress. The hem is short, and I tug it further down my thighs, cheeks flaming under his perusal. Around him, I always feel jangled up and wrong. Like a little kid playing pretend as an adult. And why wouldn't I, with his tailored shirts and his vests and his designer stubble? With his fame and his high-flying career?

That's not even the real reason he makes me feel ten inches tall.

It's because he knows my secret. What I'm really like.

"Do you have an appointment?"

His voice is rich but not warm. Let it be known: this man is not happy to see me. He's so clear about it, I catch a girl raising her eyebrow as she walks past behind me.

She probably thinks I missed a deadline. Cheated on a test or lost a library book.

The truth is so much more humiliating.

"No." I twist the hem of my sweater dress in my fingers, but his eyes drop and I force myself to let go. *I am an adult. I am a legitimate college student. I need these credits, and I can freaking do this.*

I clear my throat and wet my lips. "It won't take long, though. And I know you have a free period, so.."

His eyebrow rises. I've given away too much. I hurry to keep talking, to cover my slip.

"So I was hoping you could squeeze me in?"

Pure, unadulterated disdain flashes across his face before he schools his features carefully blank. It's too late, though. I saw it. He's confirmed what he thinks of me. A full-body cringe threatens to fold me in half, to melt me into a little puddle on the floor.

"Very well." His answer shocks me so much, I don't process it at first. I stay frozen in the corridor, my eyes locked on him, paralyzed by my own misery. Only when his eyes narrow do I realize what he said, the sentence floating through my muddled thoughts.

"Great!" I squeak, nudging past him into the office before he can change his mind. My shoulder brushes against his chest as I go, and I bite down hard on my lip.

This is such a huge mistake.

* * *

"I need English credits."

I wait until he's settled behind his desk, hands resting lightly on the arms of his chair, before I speak. Something passes behind his eyes, a darkness moving through his expression, but it's gone before it's ever really there. I cross my legs, shoving my hands under my thighs to keep from fiddling.

God. He makes me so nervous. I bet he can't believe I was ever that confident, sultry girl in the bar.

"Yours is the only class that fits my schedule."

He huffs out a laugh, leaning back in his chair. He might be laughing, but there's no real mirth in his face. I take the opportunity to look at him, to really study him, for the first time in two years. His warm brown hair is longer, a stray wave hanging over his forehead, and his cheekbones are as sharp as I remember. Under his shirt and gray tailored vest, his shoulders and chest are broad, narrowing to a toned waist. The buttons on his shirt gape slightly as his chest rises and falls.

Here, in his office, I can smell him.

"How flattering. Did it take you long to work up that pitch?"

His scent is concentrated in the small room. Or maybe it's that he smells of his things—of the lush green plant on his windowsill, and the piles of worn paperbacks, and the rain dripping down the glass.

I give myself an inner shake, forcing myself to breathe through my mouth instead. His patience is already wearing thin. I can see it in the way his eyes keep flicking to the clock on the wall. His hands tighten on his armrests like he's about to push to his feet and escort me out.

"Please." I blurt out the word into the ringing quiet of the office. Through the wooden door, the heater clunks and rumbles in the hallway. "I need those credits to graduate. Then you'll never have to see me again."

He *does* smile at that. A true smile, even if it's tinged with bitterness. His eyes find mine, tiny lines crinkling his at the corners. They make him look kind. A man prone to smiling.

I guess I'll never know.

"Now that is an intriguing prospect." He strokes one hand over his chin, watching me. "Is that a promise, Lucy?"

Lucy. We've barely spoken in two years, and certainly not long enough to repeat names. I knew he loathed me, that he recognized me, but I never once dreamed that he'd remembered my name.

Sweet Lucy. He called me that once, in the bar. The night that I kissed him in the cloakroom. Kissed him, and so much more.

I cough. Now is no time for a trip down memory lane.

"Yes. I promise—" I almost call him Gideon, but I choke back the name in time. "Just one class, then I'll be gone." I force a friendly smile, to show that I mean it.

The professor's smile fades. He leans forward, resting his forearms on the desk.

"You realize, of course, that even speaking to you is a risk to my career."

I frown. It takes me a moment to catch his meaning. Not because I'm an idiot—although my thoughts are definitely muddled around him—but because it would never occur to me to cause him any trouble.

He hates me. Fine. I can live with that, even if it burns like acid in my gut when I think about it.

I don't want any trouble. I just want my damn credits so I can graduate. I tell him so, too, my voice a little harder than before, and he nods once before turning to rummage in his desk drawer.

The paper flutters as he puts it on the desk, sliding the single sheet to me. I glance around helplessly, cursing my lack of preparation. I *always* carry a pen on campus, but I honestly never thought I'd get this far. When I knocked on Professor Warwick's door, I fully expected it to slam shut in my face.

The professor sighs. He picks up a pen and places it in front of me too. It's nice—heavy in my hand and beautifully crafted. The sort of pen given as an expensive gift.

I badly want to ask him. I want to ask so many things.

I bite my tongue.

It takes less than a minute to fill out the form, even with my mind going blank under his constant, burning stare. The top of my head prickles as I bend over the sheet, my grip growing clammy on the pen. When I finally sign my name with a flourish, I sit back with a sigh like I just finished an hour-long exam.

He gives me a funny look, but he doesn't say anything. Just

holds out his hand for his pen. I drop it into his waiting palm, praying to any deities who might be listening that he won't feel how damp my hand just got from nerves. Gideon spins my paper to face him, scribbling his own name and signature and pushing it back to me like he can't stand to look at it any more.

"Drop it to the office." He addresses the window, scowling down at the quad. Blurry shapes hurry through the rain below, hoods pulled up and folders held over heads.

The dismissal is clear. He's done speaking to me, probably forever. There's no need for us to chat in class—no need for me to raise my hand or drop by his office.

I just need these credits. I hug the paper to my chest, muttering my thanks and pushing to my feet. The chair scrapes over his floorboards and I cringe, stepping around the furniture and darting for the door.

"Thank you," I say again, throwing the word over my shoulder, then I'm safely out into the corridor. With a layer of wood and brick between us, I lean against the wall and close my eyes. My damp palms press into the cool surface, my heart thundering in my chest.

I did it. I did what I came here to do. Gideon signed my paper; I'll get those English credits.

This is straightforward win. I should be punching the air; running victory laps around the building.

So why do I feel like crying?

Chapter Two

"You got it?"

Keeley snatches the photocopied form out of my hand before I've even shrugged my coat off. She scans the paper, her dyed lilac ponytail swinging over one shoulder. She pushes her chunky glasses up her nose as she reads, her freckled nose wrinkling, then she beams at me so warmly I'm surprised she doesn't fog her lenses.

"You did it, girl!" Keeley slams into me, her hugs always a force of nature. Over her shoulder, Raine watches me, leaning against the back of the sofa, her long dark hair braided over one shoulder. Of the three of us, Raine is the quietest. The most reserved. When we were assigned as roommates in first year, she barely spoke until Thanksgiving break.

"Hi." I wave at her over Keeley's back. Raine offers a small smile, the motion shifting her nose stud. She's pleased for me, too.

"You know what this means, right?" Keeley pulls back, grabbing my shoulders. I try not to wince. It's not that Keeley's rough, it's that she's enthusiastic and doesn't know her strength. As one of the top sports science students in Llewellyn College, Keeley is stronger than half the guys on campus.

"I'm taking a class with a professor who hates me?"

She shakes me until my teeth rattle. "No, Luce! Graduation!" Keeley hollers the last word loud enough to wake the neighborhood, howling up at our apartment ceiling. She barrels into me again, hugging me until I can't breathe, but I don't push her off.

I love that Keeley's not careful with me.

"We're going to graduate together next summer, then get jobs in the city, and keep living together like we're in a sit com." Keeley steers me to the kitchen as she talks, halting us by the refrigerator so she can dig out two beer bottles. She screws off the caps and clinks them together before handing me one and swigging the other. Then she wipes her mouth on the back of her hand, grabs my shoulder, and marches me back out of the kitchen toward the sofa.

"We're living together already," Raine points out, her voice quiet. She scratches her smooth, brown cheek. "Nothing will change."

Keeley yelps, expression scandalized. I wince, grinning as I swig from my own beer. The girl seriously needs volume control.

"Of course things will change!" Keeley sweeps an arm around our apartment, nearly knocking over a bookcase. "We'll have money! Independence! We can buy whatever shit we want!"

"That's not how jobs work," I hear Raine mutter as Keeley bundles me onto the sofa. Privately, I'm with Raine on this—I'm not about to blow every cent of my salary when I finally have one. But I don't have it in me to burst Keeley's bubble, and she's so starry-eyed thinking about the future.

"I'm going to buy a beanbag," she declares. "One of those massive floor ones. And a fancy coffee maker. And a poker table."

"What's wrong with an ordinary table?" Raine picks at a loose thread on her jeans, perching on the arm of the sofa. Keeley rolls her eyes and tugs her down so all three of us are jammed on the cushions.

"Ordinary tables don't have green felt."

"So?"

"So, I want the felt. Duh."

I let their bickering wash over me, digging between the cushions for the TV remote. I switch the TV on, mute it, and flick through the channels, searching for a trashy film to watch. There are tons of sappy love movies, and usually I'd go for one of those, but something about seeing Gideon today makes me steer well clear.

I settle on a slasher movie. Something filled with jump scares and bright red fake blood. Raine excuses herself, wandering off to read in her bedroom, but Keeley stays and throws her feet in my lap.

"Why does that professor guy hate you so much, anyway?" She rummages in a half-eaten bag of toffee popcorn, her eyes glued to the screen. I chew on my bottom lip, forcing my face to stay calm.

"Dunno." Keeley shoots me a disbelieving look, so I shrug. "He caught me chatting in his class two years ago. That must be why."

"Jeez." Keeley flops back against the sofa cushions, wriggling to get comfortable. She grabs a massive handful of popcorn, dropping pieces all over herself and offering me the bag. I shake my head. "Talk about uptight." She grins around a mouthful of popcorn. "He needs to get laid."

I splutter, taking a long pull from my beer to hide the blush staining my cheeks. Keeley watches me out of the corner of her eye, expression canny.

"He's cute, isn't he?"

I shrug, the movement jerky. If I lie and say Gideon's gross, then Keeley is guaranteed to meet him and find out I'm a big fat liar. But if I tell her how gorgeous he is, how my heart pounds just thinking about him—

Well. Some things are better unsaid.

"He's okay," I hedge. "Aren't all professors kind of cute? The young ones, anyway."

Keeley nods sagely. "Yeah, you're right. It's like firemen. The job makes them sexy."

"Exactly." I laugh, relieved. No need to bare all my secrets tonight. "Plus, he disapproves of me."

Keeley hums. "Oh, hell yeah. That's a smokin' combination." She turns to me, smirking with her cheek pressed into the cushion. "You should screw him, Luce."

My face burns hotter than the sun. Keeley snickers when she sees, nudging my shoulder.

"What? Too much of a prude?"

Right. Because to Keeley and Raine and almost everyone else I know, I'm little good girl Lucy. Lucy who goes on sweet dates and *maybe* kisses by the front door. Lucy who'd never drag a strange man into a cloakroom and drop to her knees.

I scratch at the label on my beer bottle.

If only they knew.

* * *

My bedroom is dark by the time I go to bed. It's long past midnight, the orange glow from the street lamp outside pooling over my desk and bed. I have the smallest room in the apartment, but I don't mind. I'm barely 5'2". It only seems fair.

I flick on the bedside lamp, placing the class registration form on my desk. My feet throb as I drop onto my bed, finally kicking off my boots, and I rub circles into the arch of my foot.

A tiny voice whispers in my brain, wondering whether Gideon would give his girlfriend foot rubs, but I shut that thought down.

He signed the form. I got into his class. The last thing I need is to ruin it now. And what use are thoughts like that? Even if he weren't my professor, even if it wouldn't risk his whole career, I broke any chance of something between us years ago.

"Come on." I mutter under my breath as I push to my feet, tugging my sweater dress over my head. My blinds are open but there's no building opposite; no one to peer inside. And honestly, the thought makes my skin tingle.

I take my time to change into my pajamas, peeling my clothes off slowly and flipping my hair over my shoulder. First, I imagine that a pair of eyes watch me through the dark glass, then I replace the imaginary stranger with Gideon.

His deep, knowing eyes. The way they'd darken, watching me. The way he might lean closer, scratching his chin, his tongue flicking out to wet his bottom lip.

The groan that I drew from him two years ago echoes through my brain like I heard it five minutes ago. I squeeze my thighs together, yanking my pajamas on, dropping onto the bed and scrambling back to sit against my pillows.

It's late. I have to be up in five hours. I curse and snatch up the form.

His handwriting is firm. Confident. I trace the dip and curve of his letters with the tip of my finger, rewriting his name and signature. I bring the paper to my face, inhaling deeply, but maybe I'm imagining the faint scent of his office.

It smells like wood. Like paper and ink.

Not like Gideon.

I reach over and slap the form down on my desk, disappointed and feeling foolish. If anyone saw me now, they'd think I was insane. Or pathetic.

Maybe I'm both. I slide deeper under the blankets, switching off the bedside lamp. The numbers of my alarm clock glow in the dark room, and the streetlight washes the ceiling orange.

My fingers creep beneath the waistband of my pajamas. I'm aching, restless, and if I don't take the edge off I'll never sleep. This is how he's left me: jittery and secretive, my nerve endings still buzzing with the ghost of his remembered touch. I run a palm over my stomach, and it's *his* palm, or at least how I imagine it would be.

Even in the cloakroom those years ago, I never got to feel him on my bare skin.

His touch would be warm and dry, I decide. Moving steady and sure over my body, like his pen looping over the paper. One hand cups my breast, and I sigh.

I decide he would *squeeze.* Pinch and tug my nipple.

Out in the apartment, the TV's still on. The sound is muffled, but it leaks through my door. Keeley's watching an old black and white movie, everyone's accents in it old-fashioned, and I screw my eyes shut tighter to block it out. I focus on the sound of my breaths instead, drawing in and out of my nose, as my hand dips lower and finds my core.

I'm wet. Aching. Ready for him.

But I already knew that. I've been this way since he tugged his door open and I stood there blinking in the corridor this morning. Since my shoulder brushed against his muscled chest and I breathed in his scent.

I slide a finger inside.

It's not fair, really, that he can dismiss me without a second thought, that he can feel such *disdain* for me when all I want is his attention.

His gaze on me. The sound of him speaking my name. The warm slide of his palm over my bare skin.

I shiver, biting down hard on my lip as I draw out my finger and circle my clit. I toy with my nipple with my other hand, still picturing him—is that how he'd do it? The rhythm he'd set? When he reached for me that day in the cloakroom, what was he planning to do to me?

I let myself dream it. Fill in the blanks. In my mind's eye, we're back in that cloakroom, wrapped in shadows and breathing shared air. It's his turn to drop to his knees. He slings one of my legs over his shoulder, his hands skating up the inside of my thighs, then he leans forward and seals his mouth—

I come with a groan, my muscles seizing as my hips buck against nothing. I collapse back against the mattress, breathing hard, and normally this is when I'd feel better. Sleepy and sated, smug as a house cat. Instead, the need is worse than ever. It's sharp in my abdomen, a real, pulsing thing, and I whimper as I toss an arm over my face.

He spoke to me for ten minutes. Looked me in the eye. Signed a form. It's hardly pornography. Yet I'm wound so tight my heart is still racing in my chest, a cool sweat beading over my skin.

I huff, rolling over and burying my face in the pillow.

This semester is going to be torture.

Chapter Three

"You look wrecked."

My coworker Dan runs his eyes over me, his gaze lingering on the damp hair braided over my shoulder and my face bare of make up. I can't blame him for staring—this isn't like me. Most mornings I paint my face like an art piece, lingering over the exact curve of my lips with a steady hand. Raine and Keeley tease me for it, calling me their little china doll, but I just like the process. It calms me.

Nothing could calm me today. When I tried to swipe mascara over my lashes this morning, I stabbed myself in the eyeball twice before giving up. Last night's jitters didn't ease while I slept—they grew and intensified in the night, feeding on my desperate dreams.

I backed away from my cosmetic bag, waving a metaphorical white flag. If I insisted on painting my face this morning, I'd have come to work as a clown.

"Thank you, Daniel. You're as sweet as ever." I poke my tongue out at him, grabbing an armful of sketch pads from the shop counter. I weave my way between stacks of easels and tables of paint pots. The store is cluttered, a hectic mish-mash of art supplies, more like a bazaar than a New England art shop. There are jars of charcoal pieces; huge displays of jewel-toned inks; trays of pastels laid out like macaroons.

I suck in a deep breath as I go, the sketch pads swinging in my arms, smelling thick paper and turpentine on the air. My pounding heart begins to settle.

This store is my happy place.

"I've done it again, haven't I?" Dan trails behind me, scratching at the back of his neck. His blue button-down shirt is crisp and clean, the collar starched to vicious points, and his clean shaven cheeks are tinged pink. I throw him a soft smile over my shoulder.

"No, you're good. I know what you meant."

Dan isn't the first guy you'd pick for customer service. He finds it hard sometimes to pick up on social cues, and he gets overwhelmed at least once most days and has to lock himself in the back office while I deal with the customers.

He's also the most talented artist I've ever met.

"Your face looks different. Kind of tired and puffy. And your eyes look smaller. That's all."

I stifle a laugh, sliding the sketch pads on top of the correct pile. It's still early, way too early for the student crowd, and the shop is quiet except for the gentle hum of the radio and the drum of the rain on the sidewalk.

"I didn't sleep well."

That's the funny thing. I can tell Dan things I can't tell Keeley and Raine. Personal things. Secret things.

Dan knows about my solo trips out at night. I told him a few months ago, whispering to him in the stockroom as we counted off boxes of pastels. His eyebrows tracked so high up his forehead, they almost disappeared into his black hair.

He didn't judge me, though. Dan's cool like that.

"Did you go hook up with some guy?"

"No." I can't get offended. It's a fair question. But for some reason, the thought rankles me. I can't imagine another man touching me so soon after I saw Gideon.

"Did you have bad dreams?"

I chew on my lip, considering. My dreams kept me up, kept me tossing and turning. But were they bad?

"No." I turn and shrug, grabbing Dan's wrist and tugging him back toward the cash register. It took us a long time to get to this point—one where I can touch him casually without him flinching, and he can pry into my personal life. But we both started working here in our freshman year, and we've had plenty of time to grow close.

Dan and I worked a shift together the morning after my night with Gideon. For the first time that day, *I* had to lock myself in the backroom and steady my thoughts while Dan held down the fort. It freaked him out so badly—freaked us *both* out so badly—that I barely dated for eight months after that.

I haven't told Dan who Gideon really is. That he's not some anonymous man I hooked up with and turned down; that's he's a *professor.* That he controls my chances of graduation, and that he hates my guts while I sigh for him all night.

"Here." I pass Dan a new roll of receipt paper, fiddling with the cash register to replace the old one. We fall silent, working with the quiet ease of two people who know each other's rhythms.

"Something's definitely wrong." I glance at Dan and find him frowning at a bent paper clip. He sweeps it off the counter into the waste-paper bin below. "I know it, Lucy. I just haven't guessed right yet."

I could tell him. I know I could. Dan would never judge me, and he'd never break my trust. It's the kind thing to do. I can see the way the unanswered question bothers him, a line creasing his smooth forehead. He rubs one eye with the heel of one palm, his throat bobbing as he swallows.

I open my mouth to tell him, to spill it all, but no sound comes out. No words.

Maybe because *I* don't know what's happening to me. Why my body is suddenly not my own.

"Don't worry about me," I tell Dan instead, voice hoarse. "I'm completely fine."

* * *

Three days later, the night before classes start, I bundle up in two thick sweaters and crawl out onto the fire escape. Peering down between the metal bars, I can see floors and floors of lit windows and puddles of rain on the steps. There's a crushed cigarette end by my knee, clearly dropped from a higher level. I flick it off the edge and watch it spiral down into darkness.

My breaths are shaky, and when I tip my head back and exhale, it mists in front of my face like a dragon breathing smoke. I huddle deeper into my layers, my ass already freezing in my thin pajama bottoms, and squint up at the stars.

There's Orion's Belt. That's the only constellation I know, and it's fitting somehow. That of all the stars, of all the images glittering above the rooftops, I pick out the man's belt.

I smirk, digging my toe into the freezing metal.

It's still coiled in my belly. The *hunger*. The same gnawing, needy feeling that got me into this mess. The one that sends me striding out into the city at night, a sway to my hips and cherry-red lipstick painted over my mouth. Normally, I'd have taken the edge off by now—picked out a dive bar at random and found a willing partner to scratch my itch. My mom would *die* if she knew what I got up to here at college.

I haven't done it. I've let it settle inside me, get its claws in. I've let it take root. Because it's different this time—it's not an indistinct craving for sensation, any sensation.

It's for one man and one man alone.

I tuck my frozen nose into the neck of my sweater, wrapping my arms around my knees. Behind me, inside my bedroom, my class schedule is tacked on the wall above my desk. And one class in particular is circled, three times a week.

English. With Gideon.

The knowledge that I'll see him in less than twelve hours stokes my craving to new levels. I squirm where I sit, squeezing my thighs together, my gaze blurring as my eyes lose focus and I picture what he might wear. How he might look, with his shirtsleeves rolled up, and a tailored vest nipping in at his lean waist—

"What the fuck are you doing out here?" Keeley crawls out onto the fire escape beside me, dressed only in sweatpants and a zip up hoodie. She shoots me a worried look as she arranges her long limbs, pushing her black-framed glasses up her pert nose.

"Stargazing." I shrug. "I don't know what any of them are called, though."

Keeley snorts. "Sounds like you're nailing it."

She scoots closer until our sides are pressed together, but I can still feel her shivers wracking her frame. It's freezing tonight, well below zero, and she's dressed for our living room, not the open air outside the twentieth floor.

"Go inside," I scold, jabbing her with my elbow. "You'll freeze to death."

"Not until you tell me why you're being so tragic."

"I am not being *tragic...*" I trail off, seeing myself with fresh eyes. Here I am, sat bundled on our fire escape, pining after a man who loathes me. *Aching* for him as I stare up at the stars.

Yeah. It doesn't look good when I put it like that.

"Screw it." I shove Keeley's shoulder, pushing her back toward the window. "You're right. If I'm going to be pathetic, it had better involve vodka."

Keeley whoops, swinging her legs around and sliding back into our apartment. I follow, the sudden wash of heat making my cheeks and throat flush.

I peel off both my sweaters and leave them puddled on my bedroom floor.

Time for some bad decisions.

Chapter Four

- Male love interest Chapter (18/6/23)

She's hungover.

Lucy Denton. The girl who *begged* me to enroll her in my class; who made a mockery of me two years ago and has dogged my steps on this campus ever since.

Everywhere I look, she's there. Like my own personal omen of destruction. In the campus coffee shop, she's three places ahead in line. In the library, I catch glimpses of her dark waves and red lips between the stacks. She's in the corridors. The lecture halls.

She haunts my every waking moment.

And now, after all that, she turns up to my class hungover? I slam my pile of handouts down so hard on the first row of desks, a sleepy student yelps and jerks upright. He takes a paper with shaking hands, sliding the stack along to the next person, giving me a wary glance.

He's right to be nervous. I'm in a fucking foul mood.

I don't look at her outright. I won't give her the satisfaction of knowing this little ploy has got to me. Instead, I watch her from the corner of my eye, tracking her movements in her seat at the back of the room.

Of course she sits in the back. Why would she come closer? Show some respect? But that's just Lucy all over.

I clear my throat, readying my presentation as the handouts are passed down the rows. When they reach Lucy, she gives the guy who passes them to her a tiny smile. Her crimson lips curve up, her delicate hand reaching for the pile, and he hands them over with glazed eyes.

Yeah. No kidding. I can't even find a reason to yell at him—Lucy has that effect on everyone.

Even me, after all this time. God, I hate that.

"Welcome to class." I begin my lecture, flicking through my opening slides. I've taught this class for two years running now—I could deliver each talk in my sleep. I let my mouth take over, coasting on autopilot, as I drag my gaze around the room.

It's the usual selection of misfits and stoners. Type-A nerds and burly guys in sports gear. Since everyone needs English credits to graduate, this class gets the whole spectrum of what Llewellyn College has to offer. And in the back row: Lucy Denton, chewing on the end of her pencil and clearly sketching on her handout.

My grip tightens on the lectern, my knuckles paling and the wood creaking, but I keep talking in that same calm voice like nothing happened. Anyone in this room who bothered to look up from their notes and laptops would see a slightly bored professor reeling through his opening lecture. Giving test dates; detailing assignments. It's the exact same as Lucy's one and only other class with me two years ago.

Before she pretended not to know me. Dropped my class without a word and disappeared into the crowds on campus to haunt me from a distance.

Ten weeks. The semester lasts ten weeks. That's thirty hours in the same room as her. Breathing the same air, feeling her gaze land on me—

I break off, snatching for my water bottle and gulping down a mouthful of water. A few sets of eyes flick to me, then away. Not hers. I'd know if she was watching.

I clear my throat. Gather my thoughts. This should be easy, automatic by now, but she's thrown me off my game. My shirt collar feels too tight, and perspiration beads the small of my back. I roll my neck as I talk, closing my eyes, and when I open them a few female students in the front row are staring at me wide-eyed.

No. Hell no. I didn't mean to make that mistake the first time, and I sure as hell won't make it again. I glare at them each in turn, eyes hard, and they flush and look down at their notes. A whisper travels along the third row, but I ignore it. The bell's about to ring anyway.

Sure enough, the clanging metal cuts through the quiet, making the closest students jump. I click off my screen, calling out reminders for the next lecture's reading. Then I pack up my things, slowly and methodically, until the pounding footsteps and chatter fade away.

I'm not alone. I know it without looking up. I know it as surely as I know my own name.

"What can I do for you, Lucy?"

My voice sounds pleasant. Calm and unbothered. All the things I'm not right now. I pack up the last of my things and shoulder my messenger bag before steeling myself and raising my gaze.

Lucy watches me, eyes wide and cheeks pink, two feet from the raised platform. Her fingers knot together in front of her sage green dress—another damn sweater dress, a shapeless bundle of wool that's somehow the most erotic thing I've ever seen. It's like she threw on a sweater then forgot to add pants, the hem brushing over her legs mid-thigh. Her legs are bare today—she's not even wearing last week's tights—and her heeled boots go up over her knees.

I swallow, mouth dry, and look her in the eye. Her chest heaves under the green wool.

"I, uh." She's stuttering. Nervous. The sound fills me with vicious pleasure. "I wanted to thank you. Again." She plucks at her dress absentmindedly. "For letting me take the course."

"Oh?" I smile, the expression sharp. "Are you grateful? Is that why you came to the first class hungover?"

She blinks at me, shocked.

"I'm not..." She trails off. It's a relief, at least, that she doesn't bother to lie.

As if she could hide something like that from me. As if I don't know how she looks when she's tired, angry, jubilant—the knowledge shamefully gathered in glimpses over the last two years.

"I expect you to show more respect next class." She nods, saying nothing. Her mouth presses in a firm line, her eyes darting to the door like she wishes she could escape.

Too bad. She's the one who sought *me* out.

"Don't expect any special treatment," I warn her. "Our little... indiscretion two years ago will do nothing to boost your grade."

She puffs up, irritation seeping from every pore, but I don't let her speak. I stride across the platform, pounding down the steps, and walk out of the lecture hall.

Let her sit with the slight. Let it burrow under her skin.

Let Lucy Denton see how she likes it.

* * *

"Whoa, man. What's got your panties in a knot?"

I set the glass down on my desk with a thud, glaring at the man lounging against my office door frame. I completely forgot, in my Lucy-addled haze, that I'd agreed to meet Fraser for drinks.

Well. Guess I got a head start.

"Shut up." I spin around on my desk chair, swiping another clean glass off the bookshelf. I slam it down next to my own glass and the half-drunk bottle of whisky I keep stashed in my drawer. "Are we doing this or not?"

"You do know it's Monday, right?" Fraser drawls, pushing off the door frame and sidling into the room. Beckett appears behind him, his shoulders so broad he almost blocks out the light of the corridor.

I flick on my desk lamp before grabbing a third glass. No need to stand on ceremony here. These men are the closest thing I have to family these days. Ever since Harry…

No. I shut that thought down. Not because I want to forget him—*never*—but because I'm raw enough today as it is. Thoughts of my brother will have to wait until I'm steadier. Braced to handle them.

"Why the meltdown?" Becket cocks his head, crossing his arms. His suit jacket strains at the seams from the motion. He's more at home in sweatshirts and long sleeved t-shirts—the sports science department must have pushed the boat out today. First day of class and all that. I ignore his question and raise my glass.

"To Beckett's suit."

Fraser snorts and pours two more drinks before clinking his glass against mine.

"May it triumph in battle."

"May it go down in the history books." We banter back and

forth, toasting Beckett's long-suffering suit, and he rolls his eyes but toasts along gamely. The others drag chairs closer, Fraser kicking my office door closed before they collapse down in front of my desk.

"God." Fraser groans, raking his hands through his red hair before scrubbing them over his face. His piercing blue eyes peek between his fingers. "It gets worse every year."

"New basket case?" Beckett asks, flicking my stapler over with a broad finger. Fraser thumps him on the shoulder.

"Don't call them that. But yes."

As the college guidance counselor, Fraser has a front-row seat to all the trauma lurking behind the scenes. When I look out at the quad, I see students dashing through the rain or sunning themselves on wooden benches. Young people at the beginning of their lives, brimming with cockiness and potential.

Fraser sees a long parade of broken souls. They come to him as their last resort.

I like my view better.

"So why the pity party?" Beckett asks me again. Fraser looks at me too, his eyes sharp and quick.

I take another gulp, shamelessly stalling for time. When they wait me out, eyes narrowed, I clear my throat and shake my head.

"It's her. She's in my class. The girl from the bar."

Fraser pales, and Beckett crows with laughter.

"Seriously? Oh, man. You are screwed. You even *look* at this girl the wrong way, and the administration will come down hard on your ass."

"I'm not going to *look* at her," I snap. "I don't want to see her at all."

"Then why is she in your class?" Fraser asks quietly. Beckett hears the serious ring to his voice and sobers too, his broad smile fading. They exchange quick glances: Beckett's brown eyes to Fraser's blue.

I tip back on my chair, scowling up at the ceiling. There's a crack splintering through the white paint.

"She needs the credits to graduate." I drop my head, glaring at them both. "I can't stop her from graduating just because... because of *that*."

I can't even say it. If I say it aloud *here,* where Fraser works as a guidance counselor—

She wasn't my student at the time. That's my only saving grace. I had no idea she was a student at all. It's the only reason they both look at me now with sympathy rather than disgust.

"Keep your distance." Beckett holds up his palms when I round on him, ready to curse him out for saying something so damn obvious. "Just... get through the semester. Grade the papers blind. And for fuck's sake, don't ever be alone with her."

It's strange to hear Beckett be the voice of reason—he's usually a man of booming laughter and sly asides. But Fraser nods along too, his fingers tracing his stubbled jawline, and I find myself muttering my agreement.

Stay away from her. Grade the papers blind. And never be alone with Lucy Denton.

I can do that.

Chapter Five

It's one thing to stay away from a girl when she's just another body in the crowd. Before she joined my class, Lucy was a drop in the ocean of the Llewellyn College student body. Even though I always knew when she was near, my skin heating and the hairs raising on my arms, I could at least pretend that nothing was happening. That she was no one, and those sensations were all in my head.

It's a whole other thing entirely to endure three hours of her presence each week.

The first week is a blur. I get through the lectures in a daze, barely hearing myself talk, and pinch my leg behind the lectern to force myself to focus for the Q&A.

She doesn't ask any questions. She won't dare.

By the second week, I'm braced for impact each time she walks through the door. Without fail, there's the initial gut punch of her beauty. Her dark tumbling waves and her wide, gray eyes. I always think the image of her in my mind's eye is impossibly perfect—that no human woman could actually be so gorgeous.

Then she walks into my classroom and the figure in my mind's eye pales in comparison.

I'm not the only one whose heart rate accelerates when she

walks through the door. The guys straighten in their rows as she walks past, their muttered conversations forgotten. They offer her spare pens and tussle to bring her the handouts.

It's pathetic. I'd judge them for it, if I weren't just as bad.

Part of me—a bitter, vicious part of myself—wonders if she's ever bumped into any of these guys in bar cloakrooms. Whether she's dragged them into dark alcoves, or taken them home.

I shut those thoughts down. I have no right to them. I never did.

Three weeks into the semester, and I have my routine perfected. She pushes the lecture hall door open carefully, always so cautious, and tip toes on her heeled boots up the steps to the back row. Heads turn as she passes, but either she doesn't notice or doesn't care.

Lucy looks nowhere in my classes but her shoes. Her shoes, and once I start talking, the slides. Her head never twitches in my direction; I never feel the weight of her gaze.

This is the dance we're in. We're two bodies in orbit, studiously pretending the other does not exist.

It almost works, too.

She looks different today. Her usual sweater dress is nowhere to be seen, and instead Lucy wears a flippy red skirt that skims the tops of her knees. Her hair is bundled on top of her head, tied in a messy knot with a pencil speared through it. One tendril of hair has escaped, dangling just behind her ear in a glossy curl, and a black sweater hugs her curves.

She makes her usual trek to the back of the lecture hall, my eyes trailing her from the safety of the lectern. This is my only chance to look at her—when her back is turned. And no one else notices the hungry look in my eyes, because they're too busy rummaging in their bags, swigging coffee, or watching her too.

Lucy flops down into a spare seat, right in the center of the back row. There are no seats in front of her, only steps, and I can see her boots cross at the ankles. She digs in her bag, her movements robotic at first, then growing more agitated. She digs deeper, her lips moving as she curses under her breath, and it takes everything in me not to call out to her.

Your hair. Your pencil is in your hair.

It's none of my business. And sure enough, a male student leans with a pen outstretched, and she takes it with a grateful smile. He lights up, grabbing his laptop and sliding a few seats closer.

My pulse thrums in my ears. I stare down at the lectern, scratching my thumbnail over the lines in the wood. My notes are prepped and ready, spread out before me, and the clock on the wall shows that it's time to start.

I stall, swigging coffee from my thermos. Unbidden, my eyes flick to the back row.

He's in the seat beside her now, twisting his laptop to show her the screen. She laughs at something he says, nodding, and I clench my jaw so hard my teeth ache.

"Alright." I speak quietly, but the room settles. They know not to talk over me. "If everyone is ready—" I glare at the back row "—we'll begin."

I was going to assign a group project today, but I change my plans on the fly. They can write an essay for their assessment instead. A book report. Anything, as long as they work solo.

As I work through the slides, the room is silent except for the scratch of pens on paper and the rhythmic tap of laptop keys. Lucy is a pen and paper girl. She carries an A4 notepad everywhere, and it's filled with notes and sketches in equal measure. Sure enough, when I risk another glance at the back row, her head is bent over her desk and her borrowed pen sketches out long lines.

She looks up. Our eyes meet.

I duck my head, scowling at the notes on my lectern, the words swimming across the paper.

She saw me looking. She knows I watch her now.

She knows I still fucking care.

* * *

This time it's me who breaks our rule. Who calls for her to stay behind. She wanders over to the base of the raised platform, one hand gripping her bag strap tight. The other students jostle past her, rushing to their next lecture or their library date or back to their cramped dorm rooms.

Does Lucy live in dorms?

No. I don't want to know. It's none of my business.

"Yes, Professor?"

Is she taunting me? I can't tell. She must know how those words, said in her husky voice—how they affect me.

"Your hair," I grit out. She raises a hand, confused, patting at one side of her head.

"What about it?"

"Your pencil is in your hair." God, this is a disaster. Surely this isn't why I made her stay behind. Surely there was a proper reason, something I actually had to say...

"Oh. Um, thanks." She slides the pencil out of her bun, freeing another tendril of dark hair. Am I imagining the waft of her shampoo? Does her hair really smell like jasmine?

"Next time..." Yeah. That was it. I wave to her outfit,

gesturing up and down her body. "Dress more appropriately, please."

Lucy frowns down at her outfit, plucking at the hem of her sweater.

"What's wrong with it? Other girls wear shorter skirts."

Other girls aren't driving me out of my goddamn mind.

"You're distracting the other students."

Lucy scoffs. "If that's true, that's their problem."

She's right, and I know she is. In my bitterness and jealousy, I've taken a stupid stand. Her outfit is irrelevant to the other students' educations, and if they can't focus, it's their own damn fault.

By that logic, it's my own damn fault too. I sigh, pinching the bride of my nose, and wave her away.

"You're right. Forget I said that."

Lucy hovers for a moment, biting her lip, then steps forward half an inch.

"Why *did* you say it?"

I give her a hard smile. "Because I'm a fool."

"A jealous fool?" Her mouth twists into a playful smirk. For a moment, we're those people from the cloakroom again. When she breathed filthy words into my ear; when my hands roamed greedily over her curves.

I shove my notes into my bag. "An easily distracted one."

It's a confession. One that I'm loathe to give her, but I suppose I owe it after trying to lay down the law. When I look up, her face is startled, and my smile is hard as I shoulder my bag.

"Like I said. Forget I said it."

She stands frozen as I cross the platform. For the second time in three weeks, I leave her there alone, plunging back into the crowded halls, my mind spinning.

* * *

The next lecture is completely unremarkable, except for one thing.

Lucy wears jeans.

In all the two years we've existed on the same campus, I've only ever glimpsed her in skirts and dresses. At least ninety percent of her closet seems to be sweater dresses; the rest cute little skirts and tea dresses.

The jeans are new. They're not worn in yet, and the blue dye hasn't faded in the wash.

I asked her to be less… distracting, and apparently she took pity on me. The realization sends a trickle of warmth through my chest, and I allow myself to throw a brief nod toward the back row.

It's sweet of her. She's trying. She didn't have to do this. God knows it wasn't a reasonable request, and she'd have been in her rights to report me.

Instead, Lucy bought jeans—the item of clothing I suspect she hates most. She wriggles now in her seat, her nose wrinkling, her fingers plucking absentmindedly at her waistband.

I won't tell her it's a wasted gesture. That the way those jeans hug her legs looks just as sinful as those baggy sweater dresses. I'd sound insane, downright creepy, and besides—she's trying.

She's trying.

Chapter Six

The spines of the library books slide beneath my fingertips. I hold my hand out as I trail Raine through the stacks, her arms piled high with Psychology books while my own are shamefully empty.

It's not that I don't care about classes. I work hard; I do the reading. But I've never felt the *fervor* that Raine does. The all-consuming passion for my studies.

Maybe it's because I'm an art major. Books are useful, interesting, but for me nothing can compare to the feel of charcoal gripped between my fingers. While Raine pores over her textbooks, her eyes glued to each word, I daydream about running my palms over slick, spinning clay.

My hand lifts of its own accord, patting at the pencil in my hair.

Gideon—Professor Warwick—noticed. Not just that I slid my pencil into my bun, but that I couldn't find it in my bag and had to borrow a pen. He watches me more closely than he lets on.

"What was the reference number?" Raine asks, not turning her head as she walks. I read it to her again from the scrap of paper in my grip. Gideon assigned our first essay this week, and though I know how pathetic it is, I want to impress him. I'm always so freaking muddled around him, he probably thinks I'm slow. The first thing I did when I left the lecture hall was hunt down Raine and badger her into helping me find study materials.

"What's with the sudden academic zeal?" Raine pauses, scanning a shelf, then crouches to read the titles below. I shrug, even though she's not looking at me.

"I just want to do a good job."

The smirk she gives me is pure Raine. Filled with surprising, sly humor.

"It only took until your final year."

"What can I say? Better late than never."

Distantly, I hear Raine ask me to repeat the reference number, but I frown over her shoulder. For a moment then, I thought I saw…

Raine huffs and plucks the paper from my fingers.

My footsteps are muffled by wiry green carpet as I wander down the aisle, leaving Raine behind me. My heart skitters in my chest, goosebumps erupting over my forearms, but when I round the corner, he's nowhere to be seen.

He's not here. Gideon. I've gone full-blown, hallucinating-my-professor insane.

"Lucy?"

His voice is low behind me. Hushed and intimate. I jump and spin around, my breath caught in my throat. My back presses against the stacks, the shelves digging into my spine.

Gideon watches me, his eyes dark. An extra button is undone at his collar, and the muscled planes of his chest are visible through the slit in his shirt. A stack of books are clutched in one hand, his knuckles squared in a way that makes my mouth dry.

"Um. Hi." God, this man makes me stupid. He's probably shocked I'm in college at all. "I was just…" I wave a hand around. "Looking for a book," I finish lamely.

His mouth quirks. "Well, you've come to the right place."

Right. I resist the urge to turn around and slam my forehead into the shelves.

"It's for your assignment."

"I'm glad to hear it."

"I really am trying."

"I know."

I fall silent. What else is there to say? I've already made a grade A fool of myself. I throw a desperate glance out of the huge library windows, the massive panes of glass wrapping around the entire floor. The sky is darkening even though it's not even 5pm, heavy clouds bunching over the campus rooftops, and streaks of rain flash silver in the lamplight.

"Lucy?" Gideon asks. His brow is creased with concern. This isn't the first time he said my name. I draw in a shuddering breath, wiping my clammy palms against my jeans. Raine is going to see me here with him, she'll see me here and she'll *know.* The urgent hunger in my eyes will be undeniable. I won't be able to hide anymore.

There's no way I can keep being good little Lucy when Gideon is around.

People will know about me. About what I do. Where I go. About the insatiable urges I get, so unladylike, so improper, so utterly counter to everything I was taught as a child.

Suddenly the library stacks are too close, crowding in all around me. The air is stale and thin, the shadows skitter in the corners of the room, and when my fingers scrabble against the shelf behind me, I can't get a grip.

What the hell is happening to me?

Gideon says something else, his voice muffled and distant, but I push past his outstretched arm and stumble down the aisle. Raine glances up as I pass, her mouth dropping open, but I don't stop. I keep going until my palms slam against the door, the sound echoing through the quiet library as I barrel into the stairwell.

It's cool out here. Bare. The walls are all the same off-white, and black linoleum covers the floors. A window looks out onto a staff parking lot, the neat rows of cars all the same shades.

Dark blue. Silver. Black. Red. White. I count them, focusing all my attention on those cars until my heart slows and the stairwell stops spinning. After a while, the sound of rain drumming on the roof filters back into my ears, and I unclench my fists to stare at the half-moon marks dug into my palms.

"Lucy?"

Gideon stands in the stairwell doorway, the edge of the heavy door clenched tight in one hand. He frowns as he watches me, taking every detail in. My trembling fingers; my wide eyes; my disheveled hair.

For the first time this semester, I don't want his eyes on me.

"Excuse me," I whisper, taking off down the stairs. He calls after me but I keep going, no matter how insane this makes me look.

He'll think I'm crazy. He'll think I'm damaged.

He'll be right.

* * *

The student welfare office is a squat brick building with ivy climbing the walls. It's tucked away on the edge of campus, with flowerbeds and shrubs lining the short path to the door. I hurry past lines of soil and bristly green shrubs, most of the plants dead or sleeping for the winter. The rain soaks through my sweater and drips from the ends of my hair.

A sign by the entrance says *Student Support.*

Well… I sure hope so.

The automatic door swishes to the side, letting out a blast of warm air. I step into a carpeted lobby with squashy armchairs and a coffee table spread with old magazines. There's a water cooler on one side of the room, with less than an inch of water in it, and the walls are dotted with cheesy posters.

We're better together! one announces, with a picture of emperor penguins huddling for warmth on an ice floe. Another declares, *Patience is a virtue!,* and shows a butterfly emerging from a cocoon.

Yikes. I turn on my heel, ready to plunge back into the rain and take my chances. But a warm voice calls out from the reception desk, and I find myself glued to the spot.

"Are you coming in, sweetheart? We take walk-ins, you know."

The middle-aged woman sitting behind the desk smiles at me gently as I approach, my soaked boots squelching. She plucks a Kleenex from a box by her keyboard and hands it over. I'm not sure what I'm supposed to wipe, so I dab vaguely at everything.

"Um. Thanks. My name's Lucy Denton. I don't have an appointment."

"Lucy…" She makes a note in careful, looping script. When she smiles at me, her tortoiseshell glasses shift up on her rosy cheeks. "Welcome, Lucy. Would you like to speak with a guidance counselor?"

"Yes." I agree before I can over think it. I mean, why else did I run here? Healthy, happy people don't sprint across campus in a panic because they want to check out ugly motivational posters. Normal people don't lust after their professors, or freak out that they're going to be found out, and go into crushing spirals of shame. "Yes, please. Now, if that's possible."

"Sure, hon." The woman clucks and fusses, making a call and getting me to fill out a form. I do it all, her damp Kleenex clutched in my palm, and try not to look at the reflection of myself in the mirror behind the desk. My hair is straggly and wet; my mascara has smudged beneath my eyes. I'm soaked through and red-eyed. It's not a pretty sight.

The man who comes out to fetch me is tall and broad-chested. He's handsome—the sort of handsome that would make me melt if I weren't so fixated on Gideon. His red hair sweeps back from his forehead, and his blue eyes crease when he smiles.

"Come on inside, Lucy." He gestures down a corridor. "Let's talk it through."

I've never had therapy before. I guess I've always thought of it as... well, a bit weird. Something for trauma victims and crazy people. I guess I qualify.

As the guidance counselor pushes his door open, I'm braced for an office filled with bean bags and bouncy balls, or one of those leather fainting couches. Instead, there are two regular, straight-backed chairs, a low table with tissues, a jug of water and two glasses, and a fish tank on a shelf in the corner. Potted plants line the windowsill, and there's a painting of a windswept mountain on one wall.

I cross straight to the painting. At first glance, it seems no more than motel art, but on closer inspection I find layers and layers to it. Some of the colors you'd expect on a mountain—steel grays and muddy browns—have been swapped out for burgundy, teal, purple. And there are shadows, too, that don't belong on the landscape. That couldn't have been cast by the rocks.

"Do you like it?" The guidance counseor leans his desk. Drummond, the plaque on his door said. Mr Drummond.

"Yeah." I nod hard, my hair tickling my shoulders. "I love art. I'm an art major."

"What's your preferred medium?"

"Charcoal," I say at once. This is easy. If this is therapy, I'll be fixed in no time. "It's so tactile. You're not just drawing lines, you're smudging and smearing and shaping it on the paper. The marks can be clear and defined, or hazy and dreamy, and…"

I trail off. I'm not here to talk about art.

Mr Drummond senses my change in mood. He nods briskly and drops into one chair, gesturing for me to take the other. I came here by choice, I *want* to be here, yet the few steps across the room feel like walking to the gallows.

"Alright, Lucy," he says when I'm settled. "Tell me why you're here."

My chin drops, and I toy with the hem of my sweater.

"This is confidential, right?" I blurt. "I won't get in trouble?"

"As long as neither you nor anyone else is in danger, and you haven't broken any laws, then yes." He smiles. "This is confidential."

"Okay." I lick my lips. "And no one else will get in trouble either?"

Mr Drummond's smile fades. He cocks his head, his gaze penetrating.

"Who specifically are you worried about?"

My sweater twists in my fingers.

"A professor," I whisper. I'm not here to make a statement, to spill all of Gideon's secrets, but I don't know how to explain the *urges* I've been feeling without talking about him. Since he came back into my life, there's no one else. Gideon is at the heart of all my restless desire.

"Lucy." Mr Drummond frowns, muttering to himself. "Lucy. *Lucy*." His head jerks to me, his face alarmed, a new recognition in his eyes.

"Lucy," he says urgently, holding up his palms. "I'm sorry, but I can't take this appointment. I'm afraid I have some... prior knowledge of your situation."

He keeps talking, rambling about referring me to another counselor as I stare at the fish tank. An angel fish floats through the water, its pearly white fins trailing in the tiny current, bubbles floating up each time it opens its mouth.

Gideon told someone. He talked about me. He told this man what we *did*.

Did they laugh about it? Was I just some conquest to tell his friends about over beers?

"I have to go." I stand up, my chair scraping over the carpet. "I changed my mind. I don't need any help."

"There are plenty of other counselors—let me make a few calls—"

"No, thank you." I stumble to the exit.

So much for Gideon's moral high ground.

Turns out my professor is a dick.

Chapter Seven

It's not my first time skipping class, and it won't be my last. Everyone may think I'm a sweet, innocent girl who never breaks rules, but the fact is that helps me fly under the radar. I'm short and petite, with pretty makeup and stickers in my planner. I carry a sketchpad around with me and I draw for fun.

If anyone ever looked a little closer, they'd see the real me. The one that used to shoplift lip balms as a teenager; the one who takes kickboxing classes just to punch something; the one that wants a man so badly sometimes she could claw off her own skin.

Only one person has ever come close to seeing that side of me.

Gideon.

And what did he do with that knowledge? He shared it with his buddies. He probably bragged about the girl who dropped so easily to her knees. Well, I guess that means he won't be shocked when I skip his classes three days in a row.

I don't want to see him. If I do, I might throttle him with my bag strap.

I still write my assignment. I'm pissed at him, sure, but the whole point of this exercise in humiliation was for me to get those credits. So I write my essay, poring over the bibliography and double-checking my citations to make sure everything is perfect. I even bribe Raine to proofread it for me, swapping her crazy grammar skills for a warm, sugared doughnut.

Then I attach it in an email, send it to him, and shut my laptop off for the weekend.

"You're early." Dan checks his watch when I come into the art store on Friday. "Your shift doesn't start until three."

"What can I say? I was feeling generous. Plus," I jump up onto the counter, wriggling to get comfy. Boxes of soft pencils and a jar of erasers nudge away from my thighs. "I missed you, Danny."

"It's Dan." He lines up the pile of the pencil boxes, checking to make sure their edges are flush. "Don't you have class on Fridays?"

Damn.

"I skipped, officer."

I brace for the third degree. Dan is nothing if not a stickler for rules. But he surprises me, huffing out a soft laugh as he twists the eraser jar to face front.

"That means you're going out tonight."

Usually he'd be right. Usually, when my nerves are jangling under my skin, I go in search of someone to help me let off steam. My heels kick against the counter, and I weigh that thought.

Gideon's face flashes across my mind. Hurt lances through my chest.

"Nope." I cross my ankles. "Not this time."

Dan grunts, crouching to pick up a cardboard box filled with sketch pads. He starts lining them up on the nearest table, in perfect piles of even numbers.

"There's nothing wrong with it, you know." Dan addresses the piles of sketch pads. "What you do when you go out. I mean, I wish you'd take a friend or something. There are crazy people out there. But you're being safe, using—"

"Dan."

"—condoms. You don't lie to anyone. You're not hurting anybody."

For some reason, I think of Gideon again. I chew my thumbnail, uneasy.

"More people should be in touch with themselves," Dan declares, straightening up with the empty box held in front of his chest. "There's nothing bad about sex. You have nothing to be ashamed of."

"Please stop talking."

Dan grins at me, rounding the counter to add the box to our recycling stack. I stifle a smile, shaking my head, but as I sit there by the register, I let his words flow through my brain.

He's right. Dan's right. The man who—in his own words—could not be less interested in relationships sees the truth.

I don't need *therapy* because I want sex sometimes. I'm not out of control. And no good person, no one who really cares about me, would judge me for hooking up now and then. My breath gusts out of me, the tightness easing in my chest, and I tip my head back to look at the ceiling.

My awkward, antisocial friend was more help than the guidance counselor.

"Dan?" I lean back and call through the stockroom doorway. Dan sticks his head out, a smudge of graphite on his cheek. "Thank you."

He smirks.

"Just wait 'til you get my bill."

* * *

My phone buzzes when I'm stretched out on the sofa with my feet in Keeley's lap. We're watching Disney movies and eating big bowls of vanilla ice cream with cherry liqueur. In the kitchen behind us, the microwave hums and rattles as Raine makes popcorn.

I dig the phone out from between the cushions, clicking my screen on as I slurp a big spoon of ice cream.

"Holy sh—" I choke on my mouthful, screwing one eye shut as brain freeze clamps my skull. Through my open eye, I read it again. The message from an unknown number.

Unknown: You have three unexplained absences this week. Please register your sick note or other viable excuse with the student wellness center.

I stare at my phone, my tongue numb from cold. I've missed plenty of classes over the years. I've never gotten this text.

Lucy: ...Professor Warwick?

Unknown: Then again, you're well enough to complete your assignment.

Lucy: Wow. How did you get my number?

Unknown: Yes, you were certainly reluctant to give it to me yourself. It's in your student record.

There's a long pause. I snatch the bottle of cherry liqueur off the floor and take a swig. By the time I've put it back down, wincing and wiping my mouth, there's another message.

Unknown: That was inappropriate of me. I apologize.

I roll my eyes and plug his name into my phone.

Lucy: I figured you would prefer this arrangement. I do my assignments, get the credits I need, and you never have to see me in your class.

Gideon: I don't prefer it.

Lucy: Well, I do.

I wait for him to mention what happened in the library. Or to bring up my little visit to the guidance counselor. If he's close enough with this guy to tell him about hooking up with a student, I figure my walk-in appointment won't go unmentioned.

Instead, my phone stays blank. Damnably still. Apparently we're done here. I snatch for the liqueur bottle again, but thump it down on the floorboards before I've lifted it to my mouth. I've hit dial and pressed the phone to my ear before I'm even off the sofa. Keeley squawks as I kick my legs off her lap and stalk to my bedroom, slamming the door closed after me.

Gideon answers on the first ring, his voice clipped.

"Oh, so you are alive."

"No, I'm texting from beyond the grave, you dumbass."

Strangled laughter buzzes down the line. My own mouth tugs up at the corner, but I scrub at my face and force myself not to smile.

This isn't a social call. We're not *friends.* He's my professor, and he's acting like a prick.

"Where have you been?"

Is that worry in his tone? Even if it is, I don't want to hear it. Not when I can still hear his buddy's words echoing through my mind. *I have some prior knowledge of your situation.*

"Busy."

"Too busy for class? I thought you were a serious student."

I grind the heel of my palm into my eye.

"You know what, Gideon? You don't know the first thing about me."

"I know some things." His voice is dark. "I don't forget, Lucy. I have a very good memory." Shivers skate over my skin, goosebumps pebbling under my clothes, but I set my jaw.

"Yeah, I heard all about that."

"What are you talking about?"

I stomp across my room and flop down on the bed. "I went to see a guidance counselor the other day."

"After the library?" He sounds alarmed. "Are you okay?" I hate these moments. Little flashes that trick me into thinking he cares.

"Fine. No thanks to you." A sigh rattles out of me. "How many people have you told?"

"I have no idea what you're talking about."

He's going to make me say it.

"About *us*, Gideon. About the-the night at the bar." *We're in the dark cloakroom, the sounds of the bar muffled by the door, and he inhales sharply as I drag my hand down his stomach—*

This time when he mentions it, there's no sensual caress in his tone. He's pissed off, just like I am.

"Why the fuck would I tell people about that?"

"Oh, I don't know." I fling a throw pillow at the wall, where it bounces to the floorboards. "So when I go to get *help*, the freaking guidance counselor already knows my business. That's so fucking low, Gideon."

His murmur is so quiet, I almost miss it. "Fraser." Then he's speaking louder again, his voice urgent. "Lucy, it's not what you think, I promise. I… confided in a couple of friends. About a year ago. But I didn't tell them your full name or what you looked like or any identifying details, I swear."

My throat is clamped tight. When I speak, my lip wobbles. Thank god he can't see.

"Then why did you tell them about it at all? Was it—" I break off and swallow hard. "Were you laughing at me?"

"No!" He sounds horrified, almost yelling the word. I wince and hold the phone away from my ear. "No, I swear. Nothing like that. I was… upset." His sigh crackles through the speaker. "I liked you a lot, Lucy. A *lot.* And you rejected me not once but twice. First in the bar, leaving without even saying goodbye, and then when classes started a few weeks later, you acted like you didn't know me."

I splutter. "Because I didn't want to get you in trouble!"

"Oh."

Yeah. *Oh.* I filter my memories of those days through my mind, trying to see them through this new lens. We hooked up in that cloakroom, and Gideon wanted to see me again, but I told him no. And then in class, when we were both confronted with this harsh new reality, I purposely avoided his gaze. Focused on the guy sitting next to me instead. At the time, I'd been so embarrassed to see the man I hooked up with *here,* at the front of a lecture hall.

I just wanted to get away. So I ignored the professor, and after the class ended, I walked straight to registration to change my courses.

I guess I can see why Gideon's hated me so much all these years.

"Lucy..." He sounds so tired. I get it. My eyes are so heavy, I could sleep for a hundred years. Curling up on my side, I tug my blankets over my shoulder.

"What are you doing?" I mumble.

"Oh, um. I'm walking. I go walking when I'm wired. You?"

"Sleeping." My mouth quirks at his soft laugh. "You've found my Off button."

"Yelling at you?"

"No. Being nice."

A scornful laugh echoes through the phone.

"This isn't nice, Lucy. I could be so much nicer."

He's not flirting, his tone normal, but I still squirm a little on my bed sheets.

"I wish you would."

I shouldn't say these things. I know that, but I can't help it. Silence greets me, unspoken words hanging thick in the air, and I bite my lip. I'm such a fucking idiot.

But finally, he replies, and his voice is so dark with promise that my toes curl in my socks.

"Maybe I will, if you come back to class."

I laugh, lightheaded. "Okay, *Professor.*"

"Good girl." Those two words are so loaded, so laden with tension and authority, and I tip my head back on my pillow, smiling blissfully at the ceiling. "Goodnight, Lucy."

"Goodnight," I whisper. I stay on the line until he hangs up. Then I toss my phone onto the bed beside me, slam a pillow over my face, and shriek.

Chapter Eight

The lecture hall door is heavy under my palm, creaking on its hinges as I push it open. It's an 8am class and I'm fifteen minutes early—only masochists are on campus right now. The rows are empty except for one girl in the second row tapping away at her laptop and a frat guy napping in the back. He's pulled his hood low over his face, resting his forehead and crossed arms on the desk.

Gideon glances at me from the lectern as I cross to the steps. He gives me a small smile, his eyes heating before they drop back to his notes. The secret quirk to his lips stays. His damp brown hair curls around his ears, clearly fresh from the shower, and I hungrily take in his clean-shaven cheeks and tight-fitted shirt, my mouth going dry.

God. He's like stumbling on an oasis in the desert.

I check the girl in the second row, worried that my desire is written all over my face. She could hardly blame me—plenty of female students lust over Professor Warwick, and a few of the men do too. She'd probably think me just another wannabe groupie, a hormone-addled student with a professor kink.

She'd probably be right.

The thought sits uncomfortably in my stomach, but her attention is fixed on her laptop screen, the blue light reflected in her glasses. I can push that thought away for now, back into the dark recesses of my brain where I don't have to confront it.

My feet automatically lead me to the bottom of the steps, the rows of the lecture hall rising up on both sides. From down here, the lecture hall feels more like an amphitheater than a classroom. Like ancient gladiators and lions are about to burst through the doors, fighting to the death on the raised platform and knocking the lectern into the roaring crowd.

I give myself a little shake, breaking from my routine and turning into the fourth row on impulse and sliding down the bench until I'm dead center. *Gladiators and lions.* My long nights of no sleep are catching up to me. Since knocking on Gideon's door three weeks ago, I've spent more hours staring up at my ceiling and tossing in my sheets than I've been asleep.

He looks up when I place my travel mug on the desk. For a split second surprise plays over his face, his eyebrows raising, then he recovers, smoothing his features blank.

There's no need. The girl in the second row is typing so furiously that I'm surprised her laptop isn't smoking at the keyboard, and the guy in the back is snoring with every exhale.

We might as well be alone.

I bite my lip at the thought, flipping my long dark hair over my shoulder. I know I promised to tone down my outfits, to help Gideon concentrate, but when I dug through my closet last night, I couldn't resist.

I *want* to distract him. I want him to stare at me during class, losing his train of thought until someone says his name. I want him hot and bothered, tugging his shirt collar away from his neck so he can breathe better. I want him *weak.*

My legs cross under the desk and his gaze drops to the movement. Once the other students arrive, they'll be blocked from his view, but for now…

I tuck one hand under the desk and hitch my skirt up two inches. When I picked it out this morning, it was purely so I could see the look on Gideon's face. It's burgundy plaid, hanging in pleats to my mid-thigh, and there are inches of bare skin before my black socks end just above my knee.

Gideon grips the lectern. From here, I can see his knuckles pale, and maybe the wood creaks or maybe that part's in my head. I definitely *don't* imagine the way his tongue darts out, wetting his bottom lip. Nor the bob of his throat as he swallows, his gaze fixed under my desk.

I hitch the skirt another inch higher. For weeks, now, I've tried to fight this. To deny the way I feel—the powerful draw that reels me in to Gideon, no matter what I do.

When he said those words—*good girl*—in that dark, smoky tone… I was gone.

I'm done fighting this.

My teeth cut into my lip and my chest heaves as I watch him watching me. My fingertips trail from my knee up my leg, drifting over the silky bare skin. I go slowly, so slowly, imagining that it's his touch burning a trail up my thigh. Then I swoop back down to my knee, uncrossing my legs before I stroke back up again.

Gideon watches.

He always watches.

How the hell did I think he wasn't aware of me? How did I convince myself that he didn't notice me anymore; that I was safely flying under his radar? Now that he looks at me so openly, his heated gaze sliding over my skin, I recognize the weight of it. The sensation.

This is the prickling awareness I've been feeling on and off for the last two years. The sudden knowledge that someone is watching me, *wanting* me, and the answering ache that pulses between my thighs.

He's wanted me all this time. Even when he wouldn't look in my direction, when he used to walk past the art store window and not even glance inside.

The knowledge makes me giddy.

I choke back a laugh, widening my legs, and Gideon looks up at me with a smirk. It's a joke passed between us, and it's crazy how light it feels. How simple and carefree. I bite my lip as he holds my gaze, tilting my head to the side as my fingertips drift over the fabric over my underwear.

The lecture hall door slams open and I jump, snapping my legs shut. Students stream inside, eyes bleary, some muttering to each other, but none of them spare me a second glance. I flash Gideon a shaky smile, heat creeping over my cheeks, but his focus is back on his notes.

It's a taster. A tiny, delicious crumb of what we could do if no one was watching.

If we weren't professor and student; ex-lovers turned cold.

I clear my throat and flip open my notebook.

* * *

"Miss Denton?" His voice cuts through the babble of the crowd as students stream from the rows toward the exit. They're livelier now, an hour into the morning, though there are dark shadows under plenty of eyes. I push against the current, crossing to the raised platform and looking up at him.

"Yes, Professor?"

His mouth twitches. He smooths a palm over his chest then

tugs at his collar, and I suppress the urge to punch the air.

"You missed three classes last week without good reason. This is unacceptable conduct." I jerk back, annoyed, but a guy passing behind me widens his eyes in a sympathetic look. Suspicion tickles at the back of my mind, and I cross my arms as I raise my eyebrows at Gideon.

"What would you like me to do about it, Professor?"

Someone whistles as they walk past. I'm walking a fine line here, showing just enough respect to avoid punishment but making it clear that there's no warmth here. We're a mouthy student and a pissed off professor. Nothing more.

Gideon packs away his notes as he talks. "You may complete an additional assignment for extra credit. Come to my office at eleven to pick up the assignment details. And try to show some commitment this time, Miss Denton."

His tone is scathing, and when I nod and cross to the exit, the guy holding the door for me leans down and whispers, "Bad luck. What an asshole."

I turn and smirk at Gideon over my shoulder—at his possessive scowl as he sees the guy so close to me.

"Yeah," I say, loud enough for my words to carry across the room. "He needs to get laid."

The guy huffs a laugh, following me into the corridor, so I don't get a chance to see Gideon's expression. I can only clutch my notebook against my chest, my bag slung on my shoulder, and hide my smile as I plunge into the crowd. Nerves buzz in my stomach as I walk to my next class, and all through the hour of Art History.

They're the good kind of nerves. The kind that make your blood spark through your veins.

By 10:45, I'm restless. Squirming in my seat and staring at

the clock. The professor—a stately, steel-haired woman in her sixties—must think I need the bathroom, I'm fidgeting so much.

When the bell rings, I launch out of my seat, scoop my things into my arms and rush for the door.

Chapter Nine

Raising my hand to knock on Gideon's office, I get a rush of deja vu. Suddenly, it's three weeks ago, I'm convinced Gideon hates me, and I'm fogging up his bronze name plate with my nervous, quick breaths. A burst of laughter down the hall jerks me back to the present and I shake myself, tucking my hair behind one ear.

I can do this. I *want* to do this.

There's still a snide voice whispering at the back of my head that I'm pathetic and crazy. That Gideon meant it when he disciplined me earlier; that this really is just a meeting to pick up assignment details.

Oh god. Oh god, oh god. Sweat beads on the back of my knees and I rap on the door before I can freak myself out any worse. When Gideon calls for me to enter, I have to physically force myself to grip the door handle and turn it.

"Hello." His smile is sinful as he leans back in his desk chair, his shirt straining over his broad chest.

Okay. Not insane, then. I blow out a relieved breath and step inside, shutting the door behind me.

"Lock it."

I glance back over my shoulder, hand hovering over the lock. Gideon isn't watching me like a professor watches his student.

He's looking at me the same way he did once before—the first night we met, in that anonymous bar. The night we slipped away to the shadows together, knowing only each other's name and nothing else. The night I made him *groan.*

The lock clicks. A slow breath shudders out of Gideon, like he'd been holding it, waiting to see what I'd do. I spin around, pressing my back against the door, and drop my bag to the floor.

"Extra credit, huh?" I reach up and flick my hair over one shoulder, toying with the ends. "How will I be graded?"

Gideon doesn't answer. He turns and lowers the blinds over his window, blocking out the view from the quad. For the first time in two years, we're alone.

"Lucy, this..." Gideon breaks off, his mouth twisting. "I'm trusting you, here. This could ruin me."

My boots are muffled by the carpet. I cross the room in five steps, my skirt swishing against my thighs, until I come to a stop across the desk from him. It's a regular desk, a short expanse of wood, but it could be an ocean for all the distance between us.

"You can trust me." I flick at a stray paper clip. In the silence of this office, I can hear my heart thumping in my chest. "I've never told anyone about that night at the bar. Not a single soul."

Unlike you, I think, but I bite that thought back. This moment is so fragile, the trust between us the most delicate of threads, and harsh words now might snap it forever.

"Do you ever think about it?" I need to remind him. Need to make him remember why we're here: the tension between us that ratchets tighter and tighter every day until it cannot be ignored. Gideon meets my gaze, his conflicted and mine steady. I lick my lips. "I do. At night, when I can't sleep, and I'm burning hot from the inside... I think about that night."

My skirt rustles as I sit on the edge of the desk, another inch of skin bared. Gideon watches, hypnotized, and I keep talking, emboldened.

"I think about how your hands felt on me. Even through my clothes, they scorched me, and I try to imagine how they'd feel on my skin." My fingertips trail along the hem of my skirt as I talk. Gideon frowns at the motion with the same concentration as when he's absorbed in his work. "I think about how you tasted. What you sounded like. The noises you made."

His head jerks up, and I suck in a breath. Gideon's eyes are so dilated, they're almost completely black. He pushes out of his chair and I move to stand too, but he barks out an order.

"No." He rounds the desk to stand in front of me. "Stay there."

I don't know what I expected when I came here. When I sat through that endless hour of Art History, images of being bent over Gideon's desk, his hand fisted in my hair, flickered through my mind. He'd been so dominant when he told me to come to his office. So in control. So the last thing I expect is the sight of my professor dropping to his knees.

"While we're reminiscing," he says casually, placing a hand on each of my knees and rubbing his thumbs over my socks, "remind me what else happened that night, Lucy."

Ridiculously, all I can think is that the floor will leave marks on his pants. After the cloakroom that night, I had two angry red marks on my bare kneecaps.

"Um." The boldness of a moment ago has gone as quickly as it came, and I struggle for words. "I… I found you in the cloakroom."

"Yes. And then?" A single fingertip trails off the fabric of my socks, drawing a feather-light circle on my skin.

"And then…" My brain is sluggish. Muddled by the faint scent of his cologne. "Then I kissed you."

"You did. What else, Lucy?"

My cheeks flush bright red. I've never been a blusher. I'm so damn virginal in my daily life, and when I finally crack and hook up with a man… well, by then, it's too late to be shy. Plus, it doesn't feel real. It's not real life.

I can't say this. Not out loud. Not with him listening so intently. So I talk around it, alluding to it in the vaguest terms and praying that Gideon will have mercy.

"I knelt down."

He hums. "Go on."

"I… touched you."

"You did." He smiles wryly, reaching up to rub a lock of my hair between his thumb and forefinger. "Keep going." The last time he touched my hair, he buried his hands in my dark waves and *thrusted—*

"I can't say it," I whisper.

"No?" He looks faintly amused. "You were brave enough to *do* it. Where did that girl go?"

I shrug, suddenly miserable. If that's the girl he wants, he'll be disappointed. She's not real.

"Hey." A finger tilts my chin up. I stare at Gideon's collarbone, unable to meet his eyes. All of the reasons I never see a man twice… they're coming back to me now. The pressure and the sudden rush of reality and the sickly knowledge that *someone knows my secret—*

"Shall I tell you what I remember?" Gideon asks gently.

I nod, my throat bobbing as I swallow.

"I remember your mouth. Your perfect, gorgeous mouth. The press of it against my throat as you sucked bruises onto my skin; the flick of your tongue against mine; the searing heat of your mouth around my cock."

I shudder at the word. *He said it.* Out loud. Gideon said what I did.

"I remember that too," I croak.

"Good." Gideon's thumb rubs over my cheekbone. He's not touching my legs anymore. "Good. Do you remember what happened next?"

My nod is jerky. "I left."

Gideon hums again. "I remember that part differently. I remember you sucking out my goddamn soul, Lucy, and I remember reaching for you to return the favor. To make you feel as fucking incredible as you made me feel." He smiles, rueful. "*Then* I remember you leaving. Dancing out of reach like a wisp of smoke. Why did you do that, Lucy?"

I sit, frozen. Gideon watches me expectantly, waiting for a reply, but how can I answer that? How can I explain to him what I don't understand myself? That I somehow knew, that night in the cloakroom, that if Gideon touched me and walked away after, I'd crumple in on myself like a dying star?

I force a shrug. "Maybe I had to leave."

Gideon shakes his head. "That's not it." His palm lands on my thigh, the touch gentle and warm, but he doesn't move it. "Do you not like this, Lucy? Do you not like when a man uses his mouth on you?"

My ears are ringing. I shake my head to clear the sound, and Gideon takes it as my answer. He withdraws his hand, sitting back on his heels, and I snatch at him in a panic, plastering his palm back against my leg.

"I do like it. Probably. I, um. I don't know yet."

A fire sparks in Gideon's eyes. "You've never done this?"

I shake my head.

"But you want to?"

I nod.

Gideon sucks in a long breath, holding it for a moment, then gusts it out in one go. He pushes up on his knees again, both palms against my legs now, and his strokes are sure up and down my thighs.

"I'm going to touch you," he tells me conversationally, "and kiss you. And Lucy? I'm going to feel you come on my tongue."

I whimper, my heart beating so fast it might explode as Gideon nudges my knees apart. I shuffle forward to help, bringing my ass flush with the edge of the desk, and his mouth quirks in approval.

"Fuck, Lucy." His fingers hook in my underwear, dragging them excruciatingly slowly down my legs. When he pulls them over my boots, he rubs the fabric with his thumb before he places them on the desk beside me. "I've been dreaming about this for two years."

I guess I can tell, since Gideon doesn't mess around. He hooks both legs over his shoulders, spreading me apart. I'm wide open in front of him, exposed, but I don't have time to feel self conscious before Gideon leans forward and licks a stripe up my core. I suck in a sharp breath, my head tipping back, but I don't stare at the ceiling for long. I want to watch him; want to see every stroke of his tongue and hollowing of his cheeks. The sensations are like nothing I've felt before, hot and slick and nimble, and when Gideon fixes on my clit, first lapping in short strokes then sealing his mouth around it and *sucking*—my thighs shake against the cool wood of his desk.

My fingers find their way into his hair, scratching at his scalp and carding through his messy waves. Gideon's eyes flick open, his gaze meeting mine, and my mouth drops open as he slides a finger inside me. He works me, my whimpers and moans as quiet as I can make them as the sounds of students echo past in the corridor. A burst of laughter just outside the door makes me twitch, but Gideon adds a second finger and crooks his knuckles, stroking my inner walls.

It's too much. The hot slide of his tongue; his fingers delving inside me; the risk of my whimpers floating through the door. I clamp down on Gideon's hand, my thighs tensing around his head, and my hips buck as I come in wave after shuddering wave. I come so hard that I forget to breathe, that my ears fill with static, and black spots mar my vision as I fade back to reality.

Gently, Gideon withdraws his hand and presses a kiss on my kneecap before rocking back on his heels. His mouth and chin are slick, his hair rumpled, and he looks so freaking debauched that I clench again on nothing.

"Good girl." I shiver, goosebumps rippling over my skin, and Gideon smirks as he wipes his mouth on his arm. "You come just as prettily as I imagined."

He helps smooth my clothes back into place before he deals with himself. His hands are gentle, efficient, and he winds one of my curls around his finger before he drops it and stands up.

It's not until later that evening that I realize he never kissed me on the mouth.

Chapter Ten

Touching her is a high. It's a stronger rush than any drug, buoying my mood and lighting up the world around me in full technicolor. After Lucy leaves my office, shutting the door with a shy smile, leftover energy sparks under my skin.

I could run a marathon. I could scale the high rise buildings downtown.

She's brought me back to life.

When Harry died, everything and everyone around me faded to gray. That accident didn't just cost me my older brother—it cost me my hope. My faith in the world. For more than two years, I've been sleepwalking through each day, just white-knuckling through to the next.

My chest aches beneath my shirt, and I rub it with my palm. It's a good kind of ache. The promise of something new.

My steps are light as I breeze through the corridors, the crowds of students parting for me like shoals of fish. I slide my hands in my pockets and nod at them, even smile, and they look back at me like I've grown two heads.

I suppose I haven't been the friendliest since starting this job. Beckett always needles me for it, calling me a hardass. In the past, I rolled my eyes and figured he was messing with me, but maybe it was his roundabout way of telling me to lighten up.

I'm light now, alright. I'm so fucking light, I'm practically scraping along the ceiling. The scent of Lucy's shampoo still lingers in my nose; the memory of her silky skin tingles against my palms.

"What's up, asshole?" I announce when I reach Beckett's office, shoving the open door wide. He looks up from his desk, already grinning. "Another shirt? Don't tell me you've gone soft."

Beckett snorts, leaning back in his chair. His muscles bulge beneath his white shirt, visibly flexing as he moves.

"You're in a good mood."

I shrug. "It's a brand new week."

Beckett eyes me. "It's a Monday. No one likes Mondays."

I'm being weird, I know I am, but I can't seem to keep the grin from stretching my cheeks. Beckett's only ever known Grayscale Gideon, fighting through each rainy week for no other reason than Harry's memory. No wonder he's looking at me like I'm insane. I found a personality transplant between Lucy Denton's legs.

"Lunch? I'm buying." I rock on my heels, trying and failing to rein in my incredible mood. Beckett stares at me for a long moment, then gives his head a little shake before pushing his chair back.

"Alright, yeah. Hold on."

Outside, the campus is rain-slicked and gloomy, the sky dark with clouds despite the early hour. Students walk together in huddles, their hoods pulled up, picking their way between pools of rainwater.

In the summer, Llewellyn College is all kitschy food trucks and sunbathers spread out on the lawns. But through the winter months, the students' clothes barely dry out before they're caught in another icy downpour.

Beckett whistles as I hop over a puddle, shoulders back and chin up.

"Fraser's gonna freak when he sees you, man. He'll want to study you for science."

"Because I'm in a good mood?"

"Because you're in *the* good mood. The first good mood ever recorded."

"Shut up." I thump him on the shoulder as we cross the quad, more than one pair of eyes flicking over us with naked appreciation. "I can be fun."

"The battle cry of downers everywhere."

The glass front of the campus coffee shop is fogged over, and a wall of heat hits us at the threshold. Inside is the muggy warmth of bodies crammed around each table, and the buzz of conversation mixed with the hiss of steam. We fall into line, the scent of roasting coffee making my stomach growl, and I eye the cabinets of muffins and cupcakes, so sugary and perfectly formed.

Is literally everything going to remind me of Lucy from now on?

"Gid." Beckett nudges my back and I move up the line, giving my order to the barista. As she rings up my total, I stare blindly up at the menu boards, so lost in thought that I barely hear her ask for my card.

"What is with you?" I hear Beckett mutter behind me. I ignore him, paying and moving out of the way.

I almost miss her. If I didn't turn at that exact moment, she might have walked past without a second glance.

Instead, Lucy stumbles to a halt, a takeout cup clutched in one hand, her eyes wide as she sees me. The guy next to her—the geeky guy I've seen her working with in the art store—frowns at her and nudges her to keep moving.

Lucy shakes herself, darting a smile at the guy and walking forward again. As she draws level with me, she curls her mouth into a small, private smile that makes me hard as a stone in my pants.

I turn to watch her go, still dazed from earlier, my gaze dropping down to that damn skirt.

"Gideon."

Beckett's voice is a bucket of cold water. Because we're in the campus coffee shop, not some private dream of mine, and he just saw everything. Lucy stumbling to a halt; the intimate curl of her mouth; my heavy-lidded gaze after her. I'm a fucking professor, and she's my student, and he just watched me leer after her like a goddamn creep.

When I look at him, his eyes are hard. The normally jovial crinkle of his eyes is gone, and a deep line creases his forehead.

"It's not..." I struggle for words. What can I even say? He's disgusted by my *looking* at her, but he doesn't know about what we did in my office. About how I touched a student—on college property—

Fuck.

"It's not what you think," I rasp.

Beckett turns, his jaw clenched, and swipes our coffees off the counter, shoving one into my hand.

"It had better not be," he grinds out, then stalks out of the coffee shop without another word.

I linger for a moment, feeling the foundations beneath me shudder and crack. Two years, Beckett and I have been friends. We've laughed together; confided in one another. We respect each other.

Or we did.

As I make my way to the fogged glass door, his look of disgust floats before my eyes.

* * *

Beckett doesn't confront me right away. He says nothing when I join him in the quad, his eyes narrowed as he sips from his takeout cup. I hold my coffee and wait, my stomach churning too much for me to drink, and eventually he sighs.

"Come on." There's no warmth to his voice. "Let's get this over with."

He turns on his heel and strides away, leaving me to follow after, my mind screaming.

How could it all fall apart so quickly? So *easily?*

How could I let it go so far in the first place?

For a split second, I force myself to imagine what Harry would think. How my noble, kindhearted brother would react if he heard I'd done such a thing.

I push the thought away, my gut swooping. It's my one bitter consolation. He'll never see this.

I'd assumed Beckett was leading me to the Dean's office, but instead we turn down the path which leads to the Student Wellness Center.

Fraser. It makes sense. It was always the three of us, bonded together by some deeper understanding. We've never had to pretend with each other; never had to fake interest or put up a front.

Beckett's right. If I'm going up in flames, Fraser needs to be there too.

Beckett's shoulders are hunched as he walks, the muscles of his neck visibly tense beneath his short dark hair. He's always striding around campus in a single layer, no matter the weather, and today is no exception. Rain drops begin to spit down from the clouds, turning pinpricks of his shirt see-through.

"Hey, Maggie."

The center receptionist gives Beckett a wave, a phone pressed against her powdered cheek. She's used to the pair of us traipsing through her lobby, dragging Fraser out on his breaks to remind him that the world's not all trauma and sadness.

I hate that we're not doing that today. I hate that my actions are about to hurt Fraser, not help him.

The carpet muffles our footsteps as we near Fraser's office, and Beckett pauses to listen before knocking.

Of course. As far as he's concerned, I've already hurt one student. No need to interrupt another. I can't linger on that thought—that I might have damaged Lucy somehow—because if that's true I won't be able to bear it.

It doesn't matter that she came to me. That she dragged me to the cloakroom in that bar two years ago, and that she sought me out again this semester. If I've hurt her...

I'll deserve everything that's coming to me and more.

Fraser glances up when we enter his office, a faint smile fading to concern. I watch as his eyes turn calculating; as understanding dawns, then horror.

"Oh, god." Fraser tosses his pen to the desk. He scrubs a hand down his face. "Tell me you haven't done anything."

Beckett turns to me, eyebrows raised. This is the moment. My last chance to lie. I could claim it was a flirtatious glance, nothing more. A hangover from our encounter years ago, back before we were professor and student.

"I'm sorry," I say instead, voice hoarse. "She's under my skin. She has been, all this time, and now with her so near again… I couldn't keep away."

Fraser's eyes fall shut. Beckett's face pales. This is the reality of what I've done: I let the burning, all-consuming need I have for my student wipe out everything else in my life.

My friends. My career.

It's all about to come tumbling down.

And even now, beneath my choking self-loathing, I can't deny an even worse truth: that it was worth it, to touch Lucy Denton like that. To taste her; to feel her shiver and quake under my hands.

I'd go to hell a hundred times over to know how she sounds when she comes.

"I have to report this," Fraser says, his voice dull. He finally opens his eyes, his expression bleak. "This isn't something I can smooth over, Gideon. I have a duty of care."

"I know." I *do* know. I've known all along. The risks were clear, and I made my choices anyway. "I'll go now and pack up my desk. I'll leave campus and call the Dean from home."

Fraser nods, his face pained, and Beckett turns to me. There's no sympathy in his gaze.

"I'll escort you."

The pain is sharp in my chest. The lack of trust stings, it hurts to my core, and what's worse is that it's deserved.

I clear my throat. "Alright." We all hover for one more moment. But really, what else is there to say?

Beckett's right to be angry. Fraser's right to be disgusted.

And I'm right to leave.

Chapter Eleven

Harry always wanted me to be a professor. He talked about it constantly when I first went to college, the first in our family to go further than high school. He was so damn proud that I even made it that far, but when my grades started rolling in, he lost his mind.

Top of my class. Again and again. Harry bought me so many celebration drinks, it's a wonder I don't have a beer gut. And when one degree naturally progressed to a second, and talks of a teaching position began...

Harry was so fucking excited. He bragged about me to the guys at his work, saying how I was the smart one of our pair. He was always joking like that, saying I'd got all the brains, just because he was happier using his hands than writing an essay.

He was a genius, though. A carpenter by day, but the most incredible artist by night. He carved gorgeous sculptures, emotion flowing through his palms into the wood.

And then he sold them for rock-bottom rates.

That bugs me now, more than I ever thought it would. That Harry undersold himself for so long. That there are pieces of his artwork out there in the city, bought and bartered for just a few dollars.

Not every piece, though. I lift the sculpture off my desk,

turning it over in my hands. It's abstract, all flowing curves and tangled lines, but beneath all that, it's a woman's face beneath a windswept veil.

I don't know who she is. I never asked. Just one more regret to carry with me.

The wood is worn so smooth it shines, so used to the stroke of my fingertips. A throat clears behind me and I jerk back to reality, shooting Beckett an apologetic smile before I remember why we're here. My office is torn apart, the books pulled off shelves and the drawers emptied out into the cardboard box on my chair. I've told myself for so long that I'm not comfortable here, that it's a stopover, but the evidence is damning.

It's in the chipped coffee mug. The well-tended spider plant. The framed photo of Harry and me.

I made a home here of sorts, almost by accident, and now I have to leave.

"I met her the night after Harry's funeral." I don't know why I'm telling Beckett this; it's clear from the coldness in his eyes that he doesn't want to hear it. But feeling the heft and shape of Harry's sculpture in my hands has triggered something inside me, has knocked something loose.

"That doesn't make it right." Beckett leans against the wall with his arms crossed, watching me pack with grim resignation. What, does he think I'll chase after another student the second his back is turned? Doesn't he know that my downfall is Lucy and Lucy alone?

"I know." I do. Rationally, I know that. So why does something wrong feel like coming home? Maybe it's because I met her that day, but getting close to Lucy again... it's the most connected I've felt to Harry in years. To who I used to be.

A soft knock at the door makes us both tense up. My mouth

runs dry, but I don't call out. Either it's her, and she'll have to see the judgement on Beckett's face, will be forced to reckon with the consequences of our actions. Or it's another random student with a question about a test, and the whole conversation will mean nothing.

We wait in silence. I can hear the thump of my heart. Then finally a floorboard creaks outside my door and the knocker walks away.

"You can't see her again." Beckett's jaw is locked. "If you do—"

"Then what?" I toss a hardback book on my desk. "You'll report me to the Dean? As soon as I walk out that door, it's no one else's fucking business."

Beckett scrubs a hand down his face, pushing off my wall. We're both breathing hard, but weirdly he seems more upset than me. *I'm* the one losing a promising career. I'm the one who just lost his two closest friends, and failed his brother's memory.

"She won't want you," Beckett snaps. "You know what the students are like. For fuck's sake, Gideon, it's a teacher kink, not a real connection."

His words punch holes through my chest, my insides aching and raw, but I don't let it show. I school my features and place the last book in the box with steady hands.

"Let's go." There's nothing else to say. Not with his warning swirling around my head.

Is that true? I was something like that for Lucy once before. An anonymous man when she wanted a tryst with a stranger.

Is this her latest fantasy? Seducing her teacher? Being my downfall?

Beckett certainly thinks so. For the first time since the coffee shop, he looks almost sorry for me as he tugs the door open. He holds it wide as I step through, my mind racing and my arms laden with the scenery of my last two years.

He doesn't say goodbye when we reach my car. He turns on his heel and leaves.

And I shut my belongings away in my trunk, then bury my face in my hands.

* * *

I've never been unemployed before. Even as a teenager, I always had at least a Saturday job. Delivering papers, or working the cash register in the dollar store, or even sweeping up hair at the barbers.

It was me and Harry against the world, and we did everything it took to make things work. Now it's just me, fighting alone, and for once in my life, I have no god-damned clue.

Where do I go from here? Another college? A research role? Do I just say 'screw it' and take off traveling? For the third day in a row, I close down the job listings tab on my laptop, gusting out a sigh. My coffee is long-cold when I swig the dregs down, wincing at the bitter taste.

I've never made these kinds of choices before. Not without Harry. Sure, he always called me the smart one, but he was so much better. He was *wise.*

He'd know what to do. He'd know the right thing to say. I thump my empty mug down on the table, eyeing the sculpture on my living room bookshelf.

"Well?" I call across to it. Jesus, it's 10am on a Thursday and I'm losing my mind. "Any pearls of wisdom, big brother? Maybe a sign from above?"

Nothing. Obviously.

My phone chirps next to my laptop, the screen lighting up with a message. Probably Fraser again, or Lucy.

Lucy.

She deserves better than this. Radio silence. Hell, I should at least tell her I've left my job. But Beckett's words have taken root inside me, their tendrils twisting and squeezing my lungs.

What can I possibly offer her now? She's young, smart, gorgeous. I'll only bring her down.

I push away from the table, striding across the room to trace my fingers along my bookcase. It's an old habit, a trick I found soothing as a boy. My phone chirps again at the table, rattling against the surface as it starts to ring, and I work my way along to the next shelf.

After what feels like an age, the phone falls silent. Something thumps to the floor behind me.

I turn and find a paperback splayed face-down, its pages creased and faded. *Pygmalion.* A play I studied in my own college days. I crouch and pick the book up carefully, smoothing out the damage.

"Well, now." Harry had whistled when he found me reading it once. *"That's a fancy looking book."*

I'd told him it wasn't all that hard, and he grinned, shaking his head.

"One day, you'll write your own fancy books, and you'll have to explain those to me too."

I'd scoffed at the time. Figured writing was something that happened to other people. But now, I chew on the inside of my cheek, considering. Then I straighten and point at Harry's sculpture.

"Alright, but no promises." Good thing no one can see through my windows. They'd call the cops to come and have me committed. I slide the copy of *Pygmalion* back into its place, then stride back to the table.

I lever my laptop open. Boot up a word document. And start writing. Almost immediately, voices start whispering in my head that it's garbage, that it's a waste of time, that I need to find a real job, damn it.

But writing has one thing the job forums don't. It lets me forget, just for a moment.

I tune out the world, narrow in on my laptop, and barely even notice the buzzing of my phone.

Chapter Twelve

He's not in class. Not for the next day, or the day after that. Gideon's not even on *campus.* When I snap and hurry to his office between lectures on Friday, the door is locked and there are no lights shining through the frame. I jiggle the door handle, students pushing past me down the corridor, the noisy heater clanking on the wall behind me.

He's gone. I can't believe Gideon's gone.

For a crazy, narcissistic moment, I think it must be because of me—because of what we did, behind this exact locked door. That I crossed a line that day, pushed him over the edge, and Gideon would rather cut and run, leaving his whole life behind, than have to face me again.

I draw in a deep breath. Hold it for the count of five. Then gust the air back out of my lungs.

It's ridiculous. He could regret what happened between us, sure. The thought makes my gut clench, but it's not exactly far-fetched. After all, he touched me, put his mouth on me, but he didn't *kiss* me. Didn't hold me.

Maybe to him it was something shameful. A lapse in judgement and nothing more. But to *leave?* To quit his job on the spot? Something's not right.

I torture myself as I walk to my next lecture, chewing on my bottom lip and staring down at my boots. I let every grim and grisly possibility flicker across my mind.

A car accident. A terrible diagnosis. A mental breakdown.

Or it could be something wonderful—for him, at least. Like an incredible job offer, or a winning lottery ticket.

Nothing fits. If something awful had happened, wouldn't the college have let the students know? And if it was great news, and Gideon left in a blaze of glory, wouldn't he at least have said goodbye?

Maybe. Maybe not. Who knows where I stand with him? All I know for sure is the heavy pit of dread which settles low in my gut over the rest of the day. Keeley and Raine try to prod me over lunch, asking me what's wrong, but what can I say? My professor's been gone for four days and I'm spinning out? They'd want to know why, and then all my lies would come out. All the things I haven't told them.

The hookups.

Gideon. Both then and now.

I'm so deep in my own secrets, I've cut myself off from the world. From the two people who've always stood by my side.

I collapse down on the stone rim of a campus fountain, wincing as rainwater seeps through my sweater dress. All around me, students hurry between buildings, binders and bags clutched in their arms, trying to rush their time spent out in the cold and wet. A flash of red hair catches my eye, then I'm surging to my feet, tripping over myself as I hurry across the quad.

"Professor!"

The guidance counselor slows, looking around for the source of my panicked voice. His eyes widen when he sees me, guilt, conflict and pity scrolling across his features.

Oh, yeah. This guy knows what's going on. He even throws a desperate glance over his shoulder at the stone path to the Wellness Center, where he can escape my inevitable questions.

"Wait!" I yell, and he winces like he's been caught, turning back to face me properly. He shoves his hands deep in his pockets, squaring his shoulders and waiting for me with a unnaturally blank expression.

"Yes?" He asks when I reach him. "Is there something I can help with?"

I flap a hand at him. "Cut the shit." There's no time for Good Little Lucy. I lean forward, hands on my hips, weirdly out of breath, then squint up at him. "Where's Gideon?"

The guidance counselor's mouth twists. He clears his throat, looking deeply unhappy as he drops his gaze to his shoes. Suddenly, all his bluster is gone, and he's back to avoiding my eye.

"Professor Warwick has left the college."

"Yeah, no shit." I straighten up, pushing my hair out of my face. "What happened? Where is he?"

"I can't divulge—"

"Sure you can. If he's gone, why does it matter?"

"If there are issues with your new lecturer, I can refer you to—"

"Stop it." I throw my hands up. "Just stop it." The burst of anger and bravado that carried me across the quad is draining away. For a horrible moment, I can see myself from his eyes: a small, rain-damp college student with a pathetic crush on a grown man. Maybe I could tell him what happened, prove I'm not completely insane to chase after Gideon, but even long gone, I don't want to get him in trouble.

I don't want his friend to think poorly of him.

Because that's the reality. That's what I am: a shameful secret that could ruin Gideon's life. Hell—that might have already wrecked his career.

"Is it me?" Misery makes my voice shake. "Is he gone because of me?"

A muscle leaps in the guidance counselor's jaw. He rakes a hand through his hair, staring up at the dark clouds and muttering something under his breath.

Then: "Gid-Professor Warwick made his own choices, Lucy. None of this is because of you."

"That's a yes," I say flatly. He can dress it up how he likes; Gideon's gone because of me. Was there a big fallout? Did they let him go quietly? Was he upset? A thousand questions crowd up my throat.

I swallow them down. This man will never answer me.

"Where is he?" I ask again.

The guidance counselor shakes his head, expression helpless, and my shoulders slump. Of course he won't tell me where Gideon is. He probably doesn't want to see me anyway.

"Thanks," I mutter, turning on my heel and walking back to the fountain, arms wrapped around my waist. By the time I spin around and sit, the guidance counselor is gone, and I'm left there alone with the world tilted on its axis.

That's how Raine and Keeley find me, two hours later, shivering and soaked through with rain. Raine grips my icy hand, crouching beside me, and Keeley begs me to say what's wrong.

So I do.

I open my mouth, and I finally tell them.

* * *

"Come with me."

Three weeks later, Raine stands by my library table with her arms crossed. I blink up at her from the book of American painters I've been staring at but not seeing. Outside, the sky is dark, and the winter winds beat against the glass, throwing sheets of pounding rain.

"Huh?"

"You've moped enough." Raine leans over and flips my book closed. "It's time to get your shit together."

See, Raine's the quietest of our group, which people mistake for being shy. But Raine's not timid; she's just extremely private, and she has a very low tolerance for bullshit. Keeley and I don't often piss her off, but when we do, we run for cover.

I huff. "What the hell, Raine? I'm keeping up with classes. Working shifts. I'm allowed to be sad."

"Nope." She pops the 'p'. "You can't confess to a badass secret life then mope around being tragic. Where's the girl who had a fling with her hot professor? Where's that girl gone?"

"To rethink her life choices."

"No." Raine yanks me out of my chair, shoving my books into my arms. "She just needs a kick up the ass."

What I *need* is time alone. To think. To grieve. It sounds silly—we were barely involved at all—but Gideon sunk his roots deep in my chest. Somehow, instinctively, I know it will be years before I'm over him.

I should be pissed at him for that. I should call him to rant and scream.

But every time I pull his name up on my phone, I chicken out. Though I'd give anything to hear his voice, his smoky chuckle in my ear, I can't risk the call. He's ignored all of my texts so far. He'd probably reject it and block my number, and I couldn't fucking bear it.

This way, at least, I can pretend there's still hope. There's a door propped open, just by a crack.

Obviously, I don't tell Raine any of this. She already thinks I'm pathetic mess.

"If you knew where he lived, would you go to see him?" Raine's shoes clatter down the stairwell.

"Yes," I say immediately. Maybe I'm not brave enough for a phone call, but the chance to see Gideon in the flesh one more time? I'd take it in a heartbeat.

"Remember you said that," Raine mutters, pushing out of the library exit. Keeley's waiting in the quad, her arms crossed over her candy-pink sweater, and a shit-eating grin stretched over her face.

"What's up, suckers?" She waves a scrap of paper. "Turns out personal information is pretty fucking easy to come by."

"We should probably be worried about that," Raine muses. I ignore her, marching forward and snatching the paper out of Keeley's hand.

On the crumpled, rain-spotted paper, in Keeley's messy scrawl, is an address on the other side of town. I stare at it; I read it twice, three times.

"Is this it?" I ask at last. "Is it him?"

Keeley snorts. "No, we broke a bunch of laws to get you the Dean's address. Obviously it's Gideon's, you idiot."

They're both smirking at me when I look up. The paper shakes in my hand.

"You going?" Raine lifts her chin in challenge. I steel myself, pushing back my shoulders, and nod.

"Hell yeah, I'm going."

"Good." She nudges Keeley. "We'll finally get our sofa back."

* * *

The door rattles under my pounding fist. It's painted pale blue, a nice match with the dark floorboards. Gideon's building is *nice.* I remember myself, easing off on my pounding and knocking politely instead. A neighbor still pokes her head out of her door down the hall, glaring.

"Sorry," I call, shrugging. She glowers, her wiry perm quivering, but I keep knocking. I've come so damn far.

It doesn't seem like much from the outside. Three weeks left alone, then a twenty minute car ride. But to me, it's been an eternity. The longer I knock, the more panic starts to gnaw at my gut, and I clench my jaw.

Just one more minute. Then I'll stop. I'll turn around and leave, and come back another day. But I'll just knock for one more minute.

When the door yanks open, Gideon looks pissed off as hell. But his eyes widen when he sees me, the irritation draining to something like guilt.

"Lucy. God, hi. I'm sorry. I, uh..." He trails off. I lift my hand and wave awkwardly. Behind me, down the hall, the woman neighbor grumbles something and shuts her door with a snap.

Gideon watches me cautiously. It takes me off guard, before I remember that I kind of gatecrashed his apartment without warning. He didn't expect me—might not even want me here. I force a smile, even as my stomach sinks.

"Hi. I, um. I had to see you. When you left..." I break off too. God, this is harder than I thought. Gideon takes pity on me, pulling his door wide and waving me inside. I step through, blinking around me like I'm in wonderland.

Whenever I've seen Gideon before, he's been formal. Buttoned up. First in the bar, when he wore a black suit, then at college where he wore shirts and vests. Seeing him now, barefoot, in dark jeans and a t-shirt, in an apartment with jumbled bookshelves and an empty mug on the coffee table… It's a reminder. He's just a *man.* A human man, the same as anyone else.

Not the demigod I built him into in my mind—the gorgeous, unruffled professor.

A man who touched me then didn't call. A man who's looking at me now with guilt in his eyes.

"Listen, Lucy…"

I cross my arms. Something tells me to shield my chest.

"I'm sorry I didn't call sooner. I've been—"

"At all," I interrupt. "Not sooner. You're sorry you didn't call at all."

He gives me a funny look, huffing out a laugh.

"Right. I'm sorry I didn't call at all. I've been… busy, I guess. Trying to figure out some things."

"Like a new job?" I raise my chin. Gideon might want to be vague, but I want to talk about this. We lost him his *career.*

"I—yes, I suppose so. Among other things." Gideon glances around his apartment, his arms loose at his sides. He looks momentarily lost, a small frown creasing his forehead.

"Why *didn't* you call?"

Gideon looks back to me. His frown deepens.

"I just told you. I've been busy."

"Only…" I twist the fabric of my sweater dress. "I've been thinking about you constantly. Non-stop. Was that just me?"

"No, I…" Gideon's mouth twists. "I'm sorry, Lucy. I guess I didn't know what to say."

There it is. What I waited three weeks and a twenty minute

car ride to hear. The confirmation of what I've suspected all this time. I built things up between us in my head, fretting and obsessing over Gideon and what he thought of me.

And all that time, he barely spared me a thought. Because to him, I'm just a student. A silly girl. A mistake.

"I have to go." I turn and stumble for the door. Gideon reaches for me, his fingertips brushing my sleeve.

"Wait, I didn't mean—Lucy, I'm *glad* you came—" He steps around me, blocking the door. His chest rises and falls beneath the red cotton of his t-shirt. The fabric is soft and worn, moulding to the dips and curves of his muscles.

Gideon's eyes find mine: hazel flecked with gold.

I've drawn those eyes so many times. I'm such a goddamn idiot.

"Do you regret it?" I blurt out. "What happened with us?"

He pauses, and that's all I need to know. I push past him, yanking the door open again.

"Have a nice life," I throw over my shoulder, then slam the door shut behind me. I stumble to a halt in the corridor, heat burning on my cheeks as my chest cracks wide open.

There's a sound. The creak of a floorboard in his apartment. Then silence.

He doesn't come after me.

I scrub my face with my sleeve, straightening my shoulders and willing my eyes to dry. It was a mistake. *We* were a mistake.

And now it's time to move on with my life.

Chapter Thirteen

His messages start on the car ride home.

I'm so sorry.

I fucked up.

God, Lucy. Please. Come back.

That last one really makes me grind my teeth. Why should I? Why should I chase around like a kicked puppy, desperate for his attention? Gideon couldn't even pick up the goddamn phone. He couldn't look me in the eye and tell me he didn't regret us.

No. I'm done chasing him. Gideon was a dream; a fantasy. A series of stolen moments, tucked away from reality with a man who made my skin tingle and my heart skitter in my rib cage.

That's over now. I switch off my phone and bury it deep in my bag.

Keeley and Raine take one look at my expression and usher me through our apartment door. They fall into sync, going through the motions the way only best friends can. Keeley tugs me to the sofa, grabbing the throw and tossing it over my legs, then clicks on an angry playlist. Raine strides directly to the kitchen, rummaging in the cupboards then emerging with three glasses and a bottle of vodka in her hands.

"Let's do this." She slams the glasses on the coffee table,

twisting the cap off the vodka with a crackle.

"I don't need—"

"Shut up."

"Yeah, shut up," Keeley puts in, kneeling cross-legged in front of the coffee table. "Maybe you don't need this, but *I* do. We all wanted you to get your hot professor, Luce."

I snort, bitterness raging in my stomach. "Sorry to disappoint."

"So you should be."

Keeley winks, her glasses slightly askew as she holds up her glass for an inch of vodka. Her lilac hair is pulled back in French braids, but a halo of wisps have still escaped their ties, and she's dressed in the baggy sweats of the sports department.

"Cheers." I raise my glass, squinting at the clear liquid, sparkling in the glow of the holiday lights Raine strung around our apartment.

"To scandalous affairs." Keeley clinks my glass and knocks back her drink.

Raine pauses, meeting my eyes before saying, "To being brave."

I look away as I drink, warmth sliding through my sore, battered chest. Raine always knows the right thing to say. The vodka doesn't hurt either, burning down my throat and settling in my stomach. Many glasses later, when the string lights begin to blur, we lie in a heap together on the sofa.

"Maybe I'll go back to anonymous hookups." I lift an arm, drawing lazy patterns to match the cracks on the ceiling. If I don't keep one eye screwed shut, the living room spins.

"Sounds fun to me," Raine mumbles from the depths of the cushions. Keeley grunts in agreement. "If you start now, you might snag next semester's professor."

I thump her with the cushion, but I can't help cracking a rueful smile as they crease into giggles.

"Maybe," I sigh. "Or maybe it's one of you girls' turn to shock the campus."

Raine snorts. "I don't even know who I'd go for."

Keeley is suspiciously silent.

I tip my head back and close both eyes, my breaths slowing in time with the music. The rain patters against our windows, our limbs tangled and sleepy, and the crack in my chest seals up just an inch.

In and out. I count my breaths, forcing myself to go slow.

I'll be okay. I have my friends, my job, my stupid English credits. And soon, Gideon Warwick will be just another memory.

* * *

I wake to a pounding headache, a mouth drier than sand, and a phone screen lit with messages.

Gideon.

Gideon.

Gideon.

He's texted and called almost every hour since I left his apartment, except for a brief stretch of silence in the night. Something tells me he wasn't sleeping in the time; he only stopped to give me quiet to sleep.

That was unnecessary, of course. He didn't account for the vodka.

I sit up in bed, wincing at the sharp pain inside my skull. The room tilts, and my stomach flips queasily. I slap a hand over my mouth, breathing through the rising sickness.

Never again.

My phone screen is painfully bright, even on the dimmest setting. I squint with one eye, skimming through Gideon's messages. Then I brace myself, count to three, and delete them all. My phone clatters against my bedside cabinet, and I ease myself back down to a lying position with a groan. Yanking my bed covers around my ears, I burrow into the warmth and drift gratefully back to sleep.

The next time I wake, I feel about twelve percent more human. I push myself up to sit against my headboard, snatching for the glass of water which has magically appeared beside my bed. I force myself to drink slowly in measured sips, breathing through my nose and trying not to focus on the sickly lurching of my stomach. My phone buzzes against my cabinet again, and I curse under my breath as I reach for it with a shaky hand.

When I click the screen on, I'm ready to tell Gideon to take the freaking hint and leave me alone. But it's not his name this time, and disappointment slides through me before horror catches up. I toss my phone to the mattress, cursing loudly, and leap out of bed only to grip my stomach and sway on the spot, moaning. Once I'm sure I'm not going to hurl on my rug, I hurry around my bedroom, pulling a sweater dress on over my clammy, hungover body.

Behind me, on the bed, my screen glows with the message.

Dan: You're late. Are you working today?

Shit, shit, shit.

I cringe at my reflection in the bathroom mirror as I scrub my face and clean my teeth in record time. My eyes are bloodshot, rimmed with last night's smudged eyeliner, and my hair is tangled and wild as I scrape it back into a ponytail. The apartment is silent as I clatter through the living room, the other girls tucked away to nurse their own hangovers.

Shit. I've never been late for a shift before.

Our building is on the outskirts of campus, tucked down a side street filled with hipster coffee shops and tattoo parlors. I don't bother trying to hail a cab; by the time they got through the weaving one-way streets, I'd have reached the store on foot. So I half-walk, half-run, my stomach somersaulting inside me, breathing in hard through my nose and trying desperately to focus on the fresh winter air slapping my cheeks.

Dan takes one look at me and bursts into laughter. I stand in the art store doorway, gasping for breath, my hair wild and my bloodshot eyes bare of makeup. I must look like something out of a horror movie, and every time Dan peeks at me again, he descends into fresh cackles.

"Oh god," he wheezes as I stomp up to the cash register. "This is gold, Lucy. You look like something fished out of my shower drain."

I hold up a palm, the image making my empty stomach clench. I swear, I can smell the vodka fumes leaking from my pores.

"Don't. Please. Have mercy on me."

Dan snorts. "I will if you will."

Despite his teasing, despite his supposed social awkwardness, Dan takes pity on my wretched, hungover form. He sets me up behind the cash register, bundled up on a chair with a blanket around my shoulders and a steaming mug of peppermint tea. Whenever a customer steps up to the counter, Dan hustles over, leaning over me to work the register.

I get a few weird looks, but I smile at the customers blandly, blowing on my piping hot tea.

The world does not deserve Dan. He is the patron saint of hungover art students.

By the time our lunch break rolls around, I'm beginning to feel more normal again. I nibble on the corner of a cheese sandwich, then demolish a green apple before my stomach riots once more. Then I slide off my chair and try to actually do some work, walking laps of the store to straighten the shelves and neaten the displays. I make notes of the products we're running low on, and refill what I can from the stock room. When I collapse back into my chair, Dan leans on the counter with a smirk.

"So," he says with characteristic brusqueness. "What drove you to drink on a work night?"

"I'd rather not discuss it," I say primly, sipping at the fresh mug of tea he made me. I never actually told Dan about Gideon, and though I'm determined not to keep these kinds of secrets again, the thought of recounting it all now leaves me exhausted.

"Is it that professor?" I choke on my mouthful of scalding tea, shooting Dan an alarmed look. He shrugs, straightening up to put his hands in his pockets. "What? You get a funny look on your face whenever you talk about him. You're really obvious, Lucy."

God. Kill me now.

"Plus—" Dan leans over, stage-whispering in my ear, "he just walked in, and he's staring at you like the Holy Grail."

My head jerks up. I blink, hard, but he's *here.* Gideon. He stands in the art store entrance, dressed in dark jeans and a moss green sweater which clings to his broad shoulders and tapered waist. Spots of rain cling to his brown hair, and his hazel eyes are fixed on me.

"Lucy." He says my name quietly, almost to himself, but to me, it echoes through the store like he yelled it. Gideon begins to walk, weaving around the displays and clusters of bedraggled art students. A couple of them recognize him from our lectures, jerking their heads around to stare at him. Their eyebrows hitch up their foreheads as Gideon approaches the counter, their eyes dropping to check out his perfect ass in those jeans.

Jealousy slices through me, but I grit my teeth. What am I gonna do, yell out at my fellow students that only *I* can check out our professor?

Well. Ex-professor. I bite my lip as Gideon approaches.

"We need to talk." He comes to a stop in front of the counter, hands shoved in his pockets. He speaks quietly, but you could hear a spider scratching in this store, it's so quiet. Everyone is holding their breath, waiting to hear what the hot professor has to say to *me*—good little Lucy Denton. Hungover mess Lucy Denton.

I clear my throat. "I have nothing to say."

"Well, I do." Gideon steps half an inch closer, throwing an annoyed look over his shoulder. The students at the nearest display snap around, murmuring nonsense about pastels and sketch pads, but as soon as he's turned back to me, they're staring again. "You could have answered your phone," Gideon mutters.

I glare. "A lot of things could have happened."

He nods once, sharp, then forces the word out: "Please."

I chew on the inside of my cheek, thinking. If we talk here, every asshole in this goddamn shop will hear our business. I'm not ashamed of what we did, unlike a certain gorgeous prick, but that doesn't mean I want to be the center of art department gossip.

I could refuse him. Tell Gideon to leave. Move on with my

life like I promised.

I slide off my chair, rolling my eyes at Dan, then gesture for Gideon to follow me. Our stock room is in the back corner of the shop, tucked mostly away from prying eyes, and though I don't want to give Gideon an up-close glimpse of how wrecked I am this morning, I know if I send him away I'll regret it.

I need to hear what he wants. Let him say his piece. Then maybe I'll finally have some closure.

Chapter Fourteen

The stock room is cramped and shadowed, with shelves of art supplies rising up on all sides. A single light bulb dangles on a cable, and I flick the switch on as I lead Gideon inside. There's barely enough space for us to stand without touching, but I tell myself we won't be in here long. He can say his piece, then we can get out of here and go about our lives. I won't have to breathe in his clean, masculine scent too much longer; I won't have to feel my heart crack open and yearn for him in my chest.

Gideon steps in after me, pulling the door closed with a quiet snap. We face each other, our chests rising and falling with each hushed breath.

This is the story of my semester: Gideon Warwick stood within arm's reach, close enough to brush my fingertips along his sleeve, yet light years apart from me. My chest throbs, so fucking sore now I'm faced with him, and I fix my gaze on his left eyebrow.

It's easier than meeting his gaze. Than confronting the sorrow swirling in his hazel eyes.

"So what's up?" My voice is brittle and light. Falsely cheerful. In my peripheral vision, Gideon winces.

"Lucy." His voice is a caress. "I know I messed up. I should have called you. Hell, I should never have disappeared at all. I should have walked straight from clearing out my office to ask you out to dinner."

I swallow past the lump in my throat. Gideon's forehead is smooth, the skin golden, and the faint line of an old scar cuts into his eyebrow.

"Why didn't you?" I whisper. God, I hate that I'm asking him that. Even now, a sliver of hope is lodged in my rib cage, refusing to dislodge.

Gideon huffs. He's annoyed, but not with me. His bitterness, his irritation—it's all for himself.

"This job is all I've known for years. When I lost it—" I open my mouth to say something, to apologize, but he holds up a palm. "When I lost it, I lost the only thing anchoring me here. I have no family in this town, Lucy. My friends hate me for what I've done, and so they should. All I've known is teaching, and suddenly I had to figure out what to do with my life. What my purpose should be."

My arms squeeze tight around my waist. How did I not know any of this? I should have asked more questions. We should have talked more.

Like I said. A lot of things should have happened.

"The last few weeks..." Gideon trails off, dragging a hand through his hair. It sticks up at the back, messy and suggestive, and I grip my elbows hard. I will not reach for him. Not even when a deep sigh rattles out of him, and his mouth turns down. "They've been hell. I missed you so goddamn much, Lucy, like a fucking phantom limb. And every day, I wanted to go to you. To beg you to be mine, properly this time. No more secret hook ups—I wanted *all* of you. I wanted to watch you eating breakfast each morning; I wanted to hear your private thoughts and dreams. But I couldn't."

"Why not?" I rasp. God, I want that too. More than anything.

Gideon spreads his hands helplessly. "Because what can I offer you, Lucy? I'm a disgraced ex-professor. Whatever I do next, I'll be starting from scratch, and I'm too goddamn old for you anyway—"

"Stop." I lick my lips, stepping an inch closer in the cramped stock room. Gideon watches me, his pupils dilating, never mind how gross I feel. "What about what *I* want? Don't you want to know?"

Gideon's throat bobs as he swallows.

"What do you want, sweet Lucy?"

My answer is easy. "You. Just you. None of that other stuff matters."

Hope breaks over Gideon's face, and it's like the sun peeking out from behind the clouds. He looks so freaking tentative, it makes my chest throb, and I move forward another step.

My arms slide around his neck. His shoulders are tense, trembling ever so slightly, and when I rock up onto my toes and drag my mouth along his throat, a shiver wracks his whole body.

"Lucy." He says my name like a prayer, burying his face in my hair. God, I hope he can't smell the vodka fumes. "Lucy. My Lucy."

I lick the skin beneath his ear, smirking as his groan shatters the quiet of the stock room. It's like a dam breaks: one second we're teetering together, our control held in place by the finest threads.

Then we lunge as one, our bodies slamming into each other as our mouths meet. We've had our differences, but on this we're in complete agreement: we need to be closer, *closer.* Sealed against each other's skin.

A packet of soft pencils clatters to the floor as Gideon scoops me up and presses me against the shelves. A tub of erasers falls too, and a stack of sketch pads, art supplies raining down around us as we sway together, a whimper leaving my mouth.

"You're mine," Gideon breathes, wrenching his mouth away to suck bruising kisses down my throat. They're going to leave a mark. Everyone outside this tiny room will know exactly what we've done. That my professor took me against the stock room shelves, claiming me with bruises for everyone to see.

I moan, scrabbling at his shoulders for purchase, and Gideon presses himself against my aching core. He hisses at the heat he finds there, reaching down to run his palm up my thigh and tug my underwear to the side.

"These damn sweater dresses," Gideon mutters, pausing to pull a condom from his back pocket. "They've fucking aged me, Lucy. They've driven me out my damn mind."

"Good," I splutter, tipping my head back against the shelves with a laugh. That wasn't my intention—they're just comfy and cozy—but knowing that Gideon's been lusting over me? Obsessing the same way I have in turn? I beam up at the light bulb, giddy with this new reality. "You deserve it."

"I do," Gideon agrees, lining himself up with my center. He runs a finger along my core, checking that I'm ready for him, and growls when he finds me slick and wanting.

"Come on, Professor." I nip at his earlobe. "Show me what you've been dreaming of."

When he presses inside, giving me that delicious stretch and burn, my eyes roll back in my head. I've thought about this moment so many times. Played it over and over in my head, in every possible location and position. I've pictured what it would be like when he's angry, when he's gentle, when he needs me so badly he can't even speak.

This is better. So much better than anything I imagined. I can smell his skin; can breathe him in. Can run my hand up his scorching hot neck and scratch at the soft hairs at the back of his head.

"Fuck, Lucy." He speaks into the place where my neck meets my shoulder, peppering the skin with kisses. I make a strangled noise of agreement. "Fuck, you're everything."

He sinks inside me, inch by tantalizing inch. And when we're finally sealed together, my thigh muscles quaking, he rests his forehead against mine.

"I won't go back from this," he tells me, voice gruff. "I can't lose the last person I love. You're mine, Lucy. Do you understand?"

I'm nodding before he's even done speaking, my ears ringing from how good he feels. And when he starts to move, thrusting against me, I actually *sob*, pressing my face into his collarbone.

Love. That's what he said. All these weeks, I've been sure that I've gone half-mad. That I saw something that wasn't really there; made this thing between us out to be something more than it was.

I'm not mad. Gideon feels this too. The unstoppable draw between us, tugging us together no matter how hard we fight. I slide my hands beneath his sweater, raking the bare skin of his back with my nails.

"You're mine, too." I tilt my head up, speaking the words against his lips. "*Mine.*"

His thrusts quicken, his grip tight on my thighs as he holds me open, propped up against the shelves. I urge him on, wanting him faster, harder, and Gideon growls as he obliges. Already, I can feel where his fingertips will bruise my legs; can feel the wood digging into my back.

It's painful. It's perfect. And it drives me higher, winding the pressure building between my legs tighter and tighter until I can't feel my toes. I moan, tugging at Gideon's sweater, and he hushes me, reaching between us.

One flick of his fingers over my clit and I'm falling, toppling over the precipice. I cling to him, shaking uncontrollably as wave after wave shudders through me. It spreads out from my core, crackling like electricity through my body from my scalp to the tips of my toes. I clench my teeth so hard I swear my teeth ought to crack, and when I finally collapse in Gideon's arms, I feel like I've run the marathon.

He follows me swiftly, pumping twice between my legs before stilling, his muscles tensing rock hard. I press dazed kisses to his throat as he comes inside me, the warmth blossoming inside my core.

When Gideon sets me back on my feet, a thousand years later, I'm as wobbly as a newborn deer.

"Steady." He catches my elbow, smiling so gently his eyes crease, and I grin up at him like I can't believe he's real. He ties off the condom, glancing around the wreckage of the stock room before tearing a sheet of tissue paper off a pad and wrapping it up. "Sorry." He grins, shrugging. "I'll pay for that."

"Hell yeah, you will." I lean against the shelves, trying to catch my breath. "You can start with hard labor."

Gideon chuckles and sets to work, picking up the art supplies scattered around our feet and setting them back on their shelves. I watch him work, still hazy, but with a sense of peace floating through me that I don't think I've ever felt before.

He knows me. Maybe he doesn't know all my details yet, but

he knows my soul. My shadowed places and my fears. And still Gideon touches me like he can't get enough; still he shoots me those secret smiles that make my toes curl.

"Ready?" Gideon asks when he's done, tucking a lock of my hair behind my ear. I reach down and take his hand, grinning up at him when he squeezes, and finally, *finally*, he kisses me.

"Yeah," I tell him when we break apart, my head spinning. "I'm ready."

Epilogue

For the first day in months, the skies are clear. Faint wisps of cloud float above the rooftops, but above the town graveyard, the skies are bright blue. I steel myself as we walk through the wrought-iron gates, squeezing Lucy's hand in my own.

Today is always hard. No matter how much time passes, no matter how long I wait for the loss of Harry to ease, it still creeps up on me. Waves of grief drag me under, stealing my breath, and this year only Lucy's gentle hands on my skin can ease the pain in my chest.

"Where is he?" Her voice is quiet. Careful. I raise our joined hands and point down the stone path. Tombstones rise out of the grass in rows, some of them plain rectangles with their carved letters coated in moss, while other graves are marked with elaborate crosses and statues; bronze plaques and colorful wreaths.

Harry has a simple cross. My brother was a simple, understated man, and I tried to reflect that with his grave. But the lettering is perfect, the stone cleaned regularly, and there are already flowers laid at the base from my visit last week.

I've been coming more and more since Lucy and I got together. I can't explain it. It's like she's opened up *all* of me, readied me to take on the world's hurts. And I'm so glad, because I haven't felt so close to my brother since he died. I raise our hands and kiss her glove.

"I'll give you a minute." She kisses my cheek before retreating out of earshot. She's done this every time I've brought her here—given me space to speak to Harry privately.

I tell him about her. About what happened with my job. About the book I'm writing.

I think on balance, he'd be proud of me. Oh, maybe at first he'd worry, fretting over this poor student I've corrupted, but when he met Lucy he'd know it's not like that. If anyone's a bad influence, it's *her*. I hide a smile, glancing at her out of the corner of my eye.

She stands further along the stone path, her head bent as she reads the gravestones, her long dark hair whipping in the breeze. When her head jerks up and she waves, I'm confused for a second. I didn't think she'd invite her friends *here*, on the anniversary of my brother's death...

The glimpse of red hair stops my thoughts in their tracks. Fraser. I can't believe he came.

My old friend walks to me slowly, hands in his coat pockets, giving me plenty of time to compose myself. I scrub at my wet cheeks with my sleeve, sniffing hard, then throw a cautious smile over my shoulder.

"You didn't have to come." My voice sounds hoarse. Fraser shrugs.

"Yes, I did."

He comes to a stop at my side, and we look down at Harry's grave together, shoulder to shoulder. We haven't spoken much over the last few months. Not since I crossed a line that Fraser couldn't allow.

He nudges me, his voice quiet. "He'd be proud of you."

It's the closest thing I'll get to his blessing. Across the graveyard, Lucy watches us, shoulders tense. She's so damn protective of the people she loves. Like a fierce little panther.

I clear my throat. "I know. He'd like her."

Our unspoken words hang between us. There's one person who's *not* here, who's still horrified by my relationship with an ex-student.

"Beckett will come around," Fraser says softly.

"I doubt it somehow."

Fraser shrugs, his arm brushing mine. "He has his own reasons for judging so harshly," he says, cryptic as ever. I wait for him to go on, but Fraser's done talking. He digs in his pocket, then crouches and places a small but beautiful wreath on Harry's grave.

"Thank you." I scrub at my cheeks again. I feel rather than see Lucy join at my other side, her warmth washing over me. She hooks her arm through mine, leaning her head on my shoulder.

"Hi, Harry," she says quietly. I kiss the top of her hair.

Yeah. He'd really like her. And I know exactly what he'd say after meeting her, fixing me with his sly smile.

Gid. Never let that one go.

I suck in a deep breath, raising my eyes to the blue sky.

I don't intend to.

THE END

Thanks for reading Extra Credit! I hope it gave you all the best student/professor butterflies. & If you enjoyed it, please consider leaving a review!

Want more from Gideon and Lucy? Check out *Off Campus*, a prequel short story about the smokin' hot night they met. Download your free copy here: https://BookHip.com/GQCNFH

And for more student/professor goodness, check out the next book in the *Office Hours* trilogy: *Bonus Study*.

Kayla xx

Teaser: Bonus Study

I knew when I picked Sports Science that I'd be outnumbered by guys. You don't have to be a genius to predict it: all you have to do is glance around the nearest gym or sports bar. Mom warned me I was going into a male-dominated field on the day she dropped me at the airport in Phoenix, but she said it with a wicked glint in her eye. And when she hugged me goodbye, she whispered, "Keeley? My sweet girl. Give 'em hell."

A smile plays over my lips as I barrel into the Sports Science department building, raindrops clinging to my light purple hair.

My mom needn't worry. I intend to.

It's early—too early for ninety percent of the student population to be awake. My thighs are hot and aching already from my morning workout, and the thermos clutched in my hand is ready to see me through.

New semester. New module; new challenges.

Let's do this.

Apparently not everyone is so bouncy first thing on a January morning. When I push through the doors into the small lecture hall, the handful of students that are already here are slumped over the desks like wounded soldiers. I give them bright smiles anyway, peering through the spots of rain on my glasses.

One guy rolls his eyes.

Whatever. No need to be rude.

My favorite seat in this ancient lecture hall is right in the front row. After three years' worth of experimentation, I've found it has the squishiest padding and the best acoustics to hear the professor. I march straight over, ignoring the grumbles from other students.

They think I'm a know-it-all. Some kind of cheat or teacher's pet, just because I'm a girl and I beat their asses in every class.

I don't cheat. I study. I train. I work harder than these idiots even know how to.

That's not a very generous thought. I force myself to smile at my nearest neighbor as I slide into my seat. He huffs, shaking his head and digging out his phone.

Fine. I tried.

The ancient heater bolted to the far wall clunks and rattles to life. It wheezes out hot, stale air, swirling dust around the small room, and I tug my sweatshirt up over my nose.

The Sports Science lecture halls are the worst on campus. I get it—the department wants to spend all its budget on cool gadgets and equipment. Believe me, I'm with them. There's an altitude simulator that I'm dying to get my hands on.

"Jesus Christ," the nearest guy mutters, dropping his phone onto the desk. He drops his head onto his folded arms and swiftly falls asleep.

Yeah. It's kind of hard to concentrate when the room gets all hot and muggy.

It's even worse when the professor walks in.

Professor Beckett Hale is the biggest name in the Sports Science department. He's published groundbreaking research, yes, but he's also coached elite athletes to gold medals and smashed records. He eats, sleeps and breathes sport, from his short dark hair all the way down to his beat up running shoes.

I stifle a smile, peering at the cracked, worn leather as he passes. For some reason, those beat up sneakers always make my chest warm. Has no one told this man he's a legend?

The rest of his clothes are understated, too. He's in navy blue sweatpants that cling to his muscled thighs, and a white t-shirt that stretches over his broad chest. Professor Hale doesn't even look up from his phone as he crosses the room. He scowls down at the screen, a Llewellyn College sweatshirt gripped in his other hand.

"Alright." His clear, deep voice bounces around the hot room. Half the students still aren't even here, but Professor Hale doesn't seem to give a shit. He flicks a glance around the empty seats, my cheeks flushing as he passes over me, then looks back at his phone, unbothered.

"Let's get out of here." He clicks the screen off and shoves it in his pocket. When he crosses his arms over his chest, his shoulder-to-waist ratio is freaking sinful. "No lecture slides today. We're gonna run. And it's gonna hurt."

A few groans sound in the back rows, but I can't help the grin stretching over my cheeks. Professor Hale glances at me again, his scowl snagging on the way I'm practically bouncing in my seat.

I can't help it. I don't care if I already worked out this morning; I love running.

The pounding of my feet against the sidewalk. The steady thump of my heart; the swing of my arms as my hair streams out behind me.

It's freedom. It's flying. And I know before we've even stashed our bags and stood—I'm going to leave these guys in my dust.

* * *

"Class doesn't actually start for another five minutes."

My head barely reaches past Professor Hale's shoulder when I bounce over to walk beside him in the courtyard. That's saying something—I'm at least as tall as half the guys in this class. Tall and strong. No wonder they grumble when they see me coming.

"So?"

Man, he sounds pissy. Professor Hale is clearly not a morning person. I rummage in my sweatpants pocket, pulling out a cereal bar and offering it to him. He scowls harder when he sees it, shaking his head and muttering something under his breath.

"So, half the students aren't here yet." I stash the cereal bar back in my pocket. "They'll miss the lesson."

"They are getting a lesson, Keeley." Hey, when did he learn my name? I grow three inches, beaming at the side of his grumpy face. "They're learning to turn up early."

"Is that fair?" I nudge him with my elbow and he jerks away, alarmed. I keep my smile fixed in place so he doesn't see my gut sink. "They're paying to be here."

Professor Hale sighs, his long legs slowing to a halt. He checks his watch, face stony, then turns, cups his hands around his mouth and *bellows*.

"Sports Science seniors! Courtyard, now!"

A pigeon bursts out of a nearby tree. It careens into the sky, wings flapping like crazy, feathers drifting down to the paving stones. In the distance, the sound of footsteps pounding over the stone paths echoes across campus.

"See?" I shove my hands in my pockets to keep from nudging him again. "They want to be here."

Professor Hale says nothing. He watches the latecomers run to catch up, bags thumping against their backs, with a muscle twitching in his jaw.

"Maybe you should let them drop off their stuff—"

"Enough, Keeley." My shoulders slump. I back up, reaching for the tree beside the path and steadying myself while I stretch out my quads. Professor Hale watches me for a second, mouth twisted, then he turns on his heel and whistles for the crowd of runners.

It's piercing. A call to action. My heart begins a drumbeat in my chest. I shake out my arms.

We take off as one, Professor Hale in the lead, our sneakers pounding the courtyard. We jostle for position, the slower or just more patient runners dropping back while the big shots push for the front. There are two other girls in this class, one brunette and a redhead, but they're not even trying to match the boys. They run together at the back, talking quietly, and for a second loneliness squeezes my chest.

It doesn't matter. I'm running my own race. And I have Raine and Lucy back home.

A few of the cockier students practically nip at Professor Hale's heels, and I wait for him to bark out orders at them. Instead, he drops back. Moves to the side and lets one of the fastest guys take over. Professor Hale drifts back in the group until he's running at my pace, just a few students over.

A dip in the path makes me stumble, and I shake myself. What, am I gonna stare at my professor for this whole run? No way. I'm not here to work on my stupid crush. I'm here to learn. To *win.*

I pick up my pace, legs pumping easily beneath me. This is part of the challenge we've been set—we're pacing ourselves without all the details. How far are we going? What kind of terrain? Are we doing hills?

I glance over at Professor Hale. He winks.

Yeah. I figured. He told us as much, back in the classroom: *We're gonna run. And it's gonna hurt.*

I shake my head, smiling, and focus on the ground rising up to meet me. The January air slices my chest on its way into my lungs, and my blood pulses through my thighs.

I was made for this.

If they don't know it yet, they will soon.

* * *

We stagger back into the courtyard, wheezing for breath. One guy—one of the runners who pushed for the front—stumbles to the flowerbeds bordering the courtyard and throws up his breakfast. He clutches his knees as he bends over, his face flushed a bright, sweaty red.

Yeah. Pacing is a bitch at the best of times, and Professor Hale didn't give us any clues. Still, this guy should know better than to rush the starting line. I wrinkle my nose, mouth pursing in sympathy.

Sneakers thump against the paving stones as the rest of the group arrive one by one. Some of them aren't even sweaty, their faces bored and pale, while others are flushed and gasping.

I don't have to look in the nearest reflection. I know surer than I know my own name: I'm bright scarlet.

A stitch pulses in my side and I prop my hands on my hips, forcing my breathing to steady. I walk up and down, my heartbeat thundering in my ears as the final stragglers arrive. The other girls run past, offering me small smiles, and I manage a feeble wave, still too winded to speak.

Doesn't matter. I tip my head back, beaming up at the white

wisps of cloud. I won.

Professor Hale jogs in last, tailing a green-faced guy on the swim team. The professor looks completely unaffected—like he's been lounging in an armchair, not running for almost an hour. He catches my eye as he passes, eyebrow quirking, and for a second I try to picture what he sees.

Bedraggled purple hair. Flushed, sweaty cheeks. A heaving chest and trembling legs. I curse quietly, scrubbing my forehead with my sweatshirt sleeve.

It doesn't matter. I'm just a student to him, never mind my crush. That's all I'll ever be to Professor Hale: an over-eager girl.

I still want to tug my collar up to my eyebrows.

"Good work." The professor's voice echoes around the courtyard. His mouth twitches at the state of us—sucking in desperate breaths and leaning against stone walls and trees. "We're starting the semester as we mean to go on."

I bounce on the balls of my feet, my exhaustion forgotten. All the good classes are in this semester, and I've been dreaming of this for months. Advanced Physiology; the Psychology of Sport; research projects and *class freaking trips*. My hamstring twinges and I drop into a stretch, forcing myself to concentrate.

He recaps the lesson. Ties it back to training principles. And then says the words which send my heart sinking to the ground: *work in pairs.*

It's our first assignment of the semester. An important research project.

And we're working in pairs.

Look, I like people. I'm always happy to do group projects. But... a single partner? Half of these guys hate me for beating them all the time, and the others are indifferent. No one wants to partner me.

I wrap my arms around my waist as Professor Hale counts us off, digging my thumbs into my sweatshirt sleeves. At least he's giving us this small mercy—he's choosing our partners for us, saving me from the humiliation of being picked last like in middle school gym.

"Keeley." His brown eyes land on me, narrowing for a second. Then he points at the top guy in our class. "And Brandon."

Brandon groans, loud enough for everyone to hear. Professor Hale moves on, mouth tight, but it's no use pretending. We all heard. My cheeks flush impossibly redder, and I offer Brandon a strained smile. He scuffs his sneaker on the paving stones, hands shoved in his pockets.

Yeah, I'm not thrilled either, buddy.

It's not fair. If I were a guy, they'd be tripping over themselves to pair up. To have my skills and hard work on their team. But because I have boobs, I'm the enemy. The girl who's denting everyone's precious egos.

I glare at the ground, eyes stinging. And when Brandon huffs and comes over at the end of class, asking for my number, I plug it into his phone without a word.

For once, I don't feel like killing them with kindness. I don't want to tease the professor or strike up a strained conversation with the other girls.

I type in my number, hand Brandon's phone back, and take off jogging back to the classroom. My legs are like jelly, but I don't care, and I push to go faster as I weave between the students spilling out of the buildings.

It doesn't matter. I tell myself so over and over, my breath hitching in my lungs.

I'll give 'em hell.

Bonus Study comes out on 03/19/21!

Check it out here: https://books2read.com/officehours2

About the Author

Kayla Wren is a British author who writes steamy New Adult romance. She loves Reverse Harem, Enemies-to-Lovers, and Forbidden Love tropes.

Kayla writes prickly men with hearts of gold, secretly-sexy geeks, and—best of all—she's ALWAYS had a thing for the villains.

You can connect with me on:

https://www.kaylawrenauthor.com

https://www.facebook.com/kaylawrenauthor

https://www.bookbub.com/authors/kayla-wren

Subscribe to my newsletter:

https://www.kaylawrenauthor.com/newsletter

Also by Kayla Wren

Year of the Harem Collection:

Lords of Summer
Autumn Tricksters
Knights of Winter
Spring Kings

Standalone titles:

The Naughty List

Printed in Great Britain
by Amazon